TRANSFORMATIONS

Pete, and Pete as Suzy

MARIETTE PATHY ALLEN

TRANSFORMATIONS
Crossdressers and Those Who Love Them

E. P. DUTTON　NEW YORK

Copyright © 1989 by Mariette Pathy Allen • All rights reserved. Printed in the U.S.A. • No part of this publication may be reproduced or transmitted in any form or by any means, electronic or mechanical, including photocopy, recording, or any information storage and retrieval system now known or to be invented, without permission in writing from the publisher, except by a reviewer who wishes to quote brief passages in connection with a review written for inclusion in a magazine, newspaper, or broadcast. • Published in the United States by E. P. Dutton, a division of Penguin Books USA Inc., 2 Park Avenue, New York, N.Y. 10016. • Published simultaneously in Canada by Fitzhenry and Whiteside, Limited, Toronto. • Library of Congress Cataloging-in-Publication Data • Allen, Mariette Pathy • Transformations : crossdressers and those who love them / Mariette Pathy Allen.—1st ed. • p. cm. • ISBN 0-525-24820-X • 1. Transvestites—United States—Biography. I. Title. • HQ77.A33 1989 • 306.77—DC20 • 89-33484 CIP
Designed by Nancy Etheredge • 10 9 8 7 6 5 4 3 2 1 • First Edition

To my husband, Ken Allen, who encouraged and supported me through every aspect of this work. To my children, Cori and Julia, and my mother, Margaret Pathy, who accepted my unexpected absences with good grace and, I think, loved me anyway.

To the gender community who welcomed me into a private world. You have shown me that there are few limits, just unexplored options.

ACKNOWLEDGMENTS

Meg Blackstone, my editor, who had the courage and the vision.
Carol Mann, my agent.
Darrell Yates-Rist, friend and collaborator, who sees what is possible.
Jenni Burleton, who gave her devotion and shared her time, skill, and sense of humor.
Elaine Wong, whose technical contribution was exceeded only by her patience.
You have given me new life by allowing me to give birth to this book.

I'd like to thank the following for your unwavering belief in this work: Harold Feinstein, Alfredo Santana, Ed Otto, Marnie Mueller, Sue Herner, Franco Sandri, Lola Bonora and Franco Farina of the Palazzo dei Diamanti, Lanfranco Colombo of Il Diaframma gallery, Cornell Capa, Ruth Lester, Via Wynroth and Anne White of the International Center of Photography, Simon and Patricia Lowinsky, Sherrie Cohen and The Fund for Human Dignity, Kitty Carlisle Hart and The New York State Council on the Arts, Larry Frascella, Allan Richardson, Tom Cone and Karen Matthews, Philip Nobile, D. Bruce Cratsley, Jeffrey Hoone and Light Work gallery, Jim Schoonover of Van James Photography, Pamela Tudor, Donna Gray, Anne Stovell, Harold Davis, Ira Zapin, Karen Symonds, Cheryl Noonan, Renée Chevalier, Ginny Knuth, Naomi Owen, Niela Miller, Roger Peo, Lee Grant, Joseph Feury, Milton Justice, Prudence Greenblatt, Mary Beth Yarrow, Gloria Steinem and Ann Hornaday, Dr. John Money, Dr. Vern Bullough, Dr. Richard Docter, Dr. Barbara Hogan, and the friends and associates whose many contributions helped bring this book to fruition.

Special thanks to: Vicky West, who introduced me to the "secret sorority" and Virginia Prince, Ariadne Kane, and Merissa Sherill Lynn, who provided theoretical understanding and practical examples of living on the gender frontier. Without your courage and clarity, the closet doors might still be tightly shut, and this book would never have been possible.

Sugar and spice, and everything nice,
That's what little girls are made of.

Snakes and snails, and puppy dog tails,
That's what little boys are made of.
— Anonymous

Ramona and Cindy

INTRODUCTION

Dark mirrors, velvet curtains, Chopin and waltzing, foreign languages, secrets. I grew up in a Victorian household, my father, a businessman, my mother, a hostess. Both highly talented in their spheres, they were mystified by each other and by America, the new country they were attempting to conquer. I lived an almost cloistered existence, convinced that all adults made up stories about how things are and spoke in codes only they understood. From a family who saw people in terms of authority figures and social hierarchies, I was sent to a progressive school where teachers were addressed by their first names and children wore blue jeans. I reacted by not speaking in school and ended up in a dark, wood-paneled room with a child psychologist who seemed to accuse me of not knowing the difference between a boy and a girl.

In high school, I read Margaret Mead and was overwhelmed by the discovery that the human family can organize itself to fit any pattern and each culture can define for itself the roles of men and women. Through Mead's work, I saw that the study of sexual and societal roles can itself be a way of life.

In New Orleans, 1978, on the last day of Mardi Gras, I went to my hotel dining room for breakfast and was confronted by a roomful of figures in long sequined dresses, butterfly eyelashes, and cascading hairpieces. After breakfast, as if on cue, the group lined up around the hotel swimming pool, striking poses. I looked through my camera lens. Each of them was focused in a different direction, except for one person wearing a green lamé dress who looked back at me, calmly and directly. It was as if I were seeing into someone's soul, unburdened by masculinity or feminity, as if in covering her male anatomy with a beautiful dress, her full humanity was present. I reexperienced the relief I'd found reading Mead's work and entered the world of Vicky West.

Through Vicky, I became aware of the full spectrum of the transgendered world: crossdressers, transsexuals, and drag artists, among others. I witnessed the sensual, artistic, exhibitionistic elements of dressing: the pleasure Vicky experienced in creating her look, in expressing herself, in being admired, and in leaving behind, however temporarily, the responsibilities and burdens of Kurt's world.

Vicky and I attended Fantasia Fair, an annual convention for crossdressers and their wives or partners. There I encountered a revolutionary idea. I learned that anatomy, sexual preference, and gender roles are not bound together like some immutable pretzel but are separate choices. We are born male or female, but masculinity and femininity are personal expressions. With the breaking apart of this pretzel, an exhilarating expansion of freedom is possible, even though in the desire to find release from the straitjacket of a strictly defined masculine role, many adopt equally defined feminine stereotypes. Some reach a fusion of the two. From this may come the ability to see it *all* as illusion: a rite of passage out of the tyranny of sexual stereotypes altogether.

Not on some remote island, yet equally hidden from the mainstream, 3 to 5 percent of the male population of the United States wears women's clothing, at least occasionally. From corporation presidents to construction workers, they represent the full range of American society. They live in the fanciest suburbs and the toughest barrios. They teach Sunday school, lead Boy Scout troops, and are members of Kiwanis clubs. The great majority are heterosexual and are husbands, fathers, and grandfathers. Theories for transgendered behavior range from genetic predisposition, in-utero hormonal imbalance, frustration with male role constrictions, environmental influences, to boredom with the limitations of men's clothing. But no one knows the reasons for sure, and the mystery adds to the fascination.

The instant I meet a member of the gender community, I am privy to his deepest, darkest secret. In wearing the clothing of the opposite sex, that person becomes naked, transparent, and we experience an intoxicating intimacy. I am given entry not only to the struggle within, but to what it is like to live as a man in America. I poach in that world, glimpsing life in a trench in Vietnam, or the lobbying for a vote in Albany. I may never know what it feels like to be a man, but I come closest when some of my best girlfriends tell me about *their* life as men. To withstand these "masculine" challenges, they may depend on their feminine creations to survive. This creation is often seen as a kinder, more sympathetic, more charming person who has easier access to feelings and a greater ability to enjoy life.

The people in this book live in drama: one foot in conventional, patriarchal society, and the other in a secret world of exploration of sex and gender role. They are in the vanguard of men's liberation, not necessarily because they have a choice, but because it is a part of their nature. After much struggle, they may come to see the positive side of this life. As one person puts it: "The shrinks may call it 'gender dysphoria,' but for some of us, it's gender 'euphoria,' and we're not going to apologize anymore!"

These are people who question gender roles not merely with their minds but with their lives. I see them as heroic because they confront what most of us keep hidden in our innermost fantasies—if we allow ourselves even that much freedom. Their struggles don't fit the old pictures of lonely figures in murky bars, back streets, and rundown hotel rooms. To depict them where they belong, in the daylight of daily life, rich in relationships with spouses, children, siblings, parents, and friends is my tribute to their courage.

At Fantasia Fair, the conga line flies across the floor, sweeping everyone along in Dionysian ecstasy. It is a folk dance of acceptance where the boundaries of age, religion, race, social position, and gender roles are irrelevant. Then comes "Old Cape Cod," a ballad, the last of the evening. Couples, trios, groups dance together. Kay and Brenda dance, arms around each other, their heads buried in each other's shoulders. They love each other, but they are not lovers. It is a love without strings or demands, a love without sex or gender, an invention. Noah's Ark has been replaced for a moment.

TRANSFORMATIONS

Ted, and Ted as Linda

*Samantha—Banker from Oklahoma,
keeps a trailer for her wardrobe*

Alice at Frederick's of Hollywood

Barbie Sue—at a vintage clothing store

Kay—Telecommunications Administrator

OVERLEAF: *Pajama party at Fantasia Fair —a rite of passage for teenage girls*

Michelle and Betty Ann—a Doctor and a Business Writer, at the beauty parlor. Michelle: "I love women so much that sometimes I want to be one!"

*Jane—British Government Official and Marathon Runner.
She says: "Jane relaxes on the beach but wonders how Jim will handle
those labor relations problems in London the following Monday!"*

Elaine W.—Holding baby April for the first time

Carol—Artist. Her passion for shoes began with "Mary Janes"

*Elaine H.—Designer/Inventor/Researcher.
"I like to travel. In many respects my crossdressing is
just traveling in another dimension."*

*Vanessa—Discovered there were other crossdressers
from article in* Playboy *at age 26;
packed VW bug and drove from Corpus Christi to Provincetown*

Pam and his sister Marie

Terry—Social Worker

Liz and her mate Jyneen. Liz: "Jyneen is more sensitive to my needs than John. I cherish the moments she emerges and becomes the witty bitch."

At a scarf-tying class at Fantasia Fair

CINDY

My mother was a square dancer. The feel of the petticoats, the sound of the skirts rustling against the nylons, that's what got to me. I have an indelible image of my parents standing, talking to each other, my mother holding my infant sister. I am looking up at them, wanting to be recognized, to be acknowledged, but the only contact I get is to hold the hem of my mother's skirt.

It is difficult to describe how overwhelmingly awful you feel when you know, absolutely know, that you are fundamentally different from the people all around you. To feel all alone in a world filled with people. Unable to talk to your parents, your siblings, or friends because you are crazy. I grew up believing this. From the time I was five, until eighteen, it was my firm, unflagging belief that I was only moments away from being institutionalized.

Long before I knew what a crossdresser was, I thought that I had schizophrenia. How else could I explain why whenever I saw a woman, my first reaction was not to who she was or her physical appearance but, rather, to her clothing? My immediate fantasy was about what it would be like to wear clothes and look like her. Clearly there was another person inside that wanted to do this awful thing.

Even more difficult to describe is how I felt in 1966 while a freshman in college when I read Havelock Ellis's description of what he called eonism. A condition which involved the desire of heterosexual males to dress as women. The volume at the university may still have the pages stuck together with my tears. That moved me out of the freak category and into a subset of humanity. A subset that it took another twelve years to make contact with.

During those twelve years, I was married, divorced, and then ran off with a woman who helped me make contact first with myself, and later with other crossdressers. She encouraged me to attend my first crossdresser convention. So, at the age of thirty-two, I ventured out into the world for the first time fully attired as a woman. I came out of the closet at warp speed. There was no stopping me. I became involved in various organizations, and was the hostess for crossdresser parties. I started electrolysis. I became Frankenstein's monster. My girlfriend lost control. I was no longer her life-size Barbie doll. I dressed myself. I went out alone.

I had found Cindy and lost myself. I was on the fast track to making permanent drastic changes to my life, convinced that I could live full-time as a woman. I could live my fantasy without limit, without end. Some days I still think about that possibility. It will always be an option that is open to me. An alternative path.

Today I have a wonderful marriage, an understanding wife, and all kinds of friends whom I can talk to. Being a crossdresser is one of life's gifts; it helped me understand who we all are—human beings engaged on a journey that has no clear beginning or a definite end.

ELAYNE

Last night I sat in a car with two crossdressers and held hands. Although we talked only about petty things, we touched. I can express my inner self as Wayne, but when I'm being Elayne, a few more bricks disappear. When I looked into Diane's eyes, she looked right back into mine, but earlier, when I talked to Ed [Diane], he couldn't look at me. We spoke to the side of each other. But Diane and I didn't speak *to* each other, we spoke *within* each other.

    I knew there was something different about me from the time I was six years old and I put on my sister's silk pajamas. They felt so good, but I was scolded and scoffed at. I grew up in a very conservative, redneck area of Iowa where "women were women and men were men." All through my childhood I wore black and white or muted plaid. When I was given crayons, I dared use only the black and white ones. I was so afraid of using color and being perceived as different.

    I looked all over for information on crossdressing. I finally found something in Ann Landers—she told a wife that it was okay for her husband to wear her clothes. When I read that, I knew there were others like me. I still have that column—it has turned yellow!

    When I'm dressed as Elayne, my son Ryan and I sometimes go for a ride through the woods and farms on our bicycles, and I'm sure most of the people who see us assume I'm his mother. I've always dressed around the kids. When they get older, maybe they'll tell their friends. I won't hide my crossdressing. I won't flaunt it either.

Wayne at work in advertising

Ryan and his father, Elayne

Elayne and daughter Sally:
"I fantasize about having a baby and being pregnant."

I don't feel particularly masculine. I tend to see men as hairy and fuzzy and bulky and aggressive. Men are dirty, and they don't know how to take care of themselves. I wouldn't want to have sex with a man.

Girls are usually encouraged to do the softer things, but if a boy starts into that softer area, he's held back. *Why should women have all the experiences in life?* I fantasized about having a baby and being pregnant, especially when Kaye was. If it were possible, I'd like to have a child. I'd be first in line to be the prototype mother-father! I'd like to have breasts and have a baby suckle at my nipple. Kaye has beautiful, wonderful breasts. It's fun for her to lie on her back on top of me, and I can put my arms around her and feel the fantasy. She becomes part of me.

Elayne with daughter Sally, painting twenty nails pink

KAYE (ELAYNE'S WIFE)

Sometimes I find Elayne too pretty and overpowering. Sometimes I feel I'm married to two people. I like them both. They have different auras. Elayne is a different kind of outgoing. If I'm feeling good about myself, I find Elayne easier to take.

When I first heard about his crossdressing, I thought it was no big deal. What's so strange about that? I even assisted him in making a dress. At first I just thought he likes to wear women's clothes because they're prettier. Now I see it's also because it enables him to get into a different space, where he is more conscious of the feminine side of himself and can make it more accessible. I don't think crossdressers should be seen any differently from artists or people who set fads.

I think Wayne's crossdressing has been, for the most part, a good learning experience for the children. It could make them more accepting of other people. Ryan climbs trees, but he also works with needlepoint. Sometimes I wonder if there'll be a backlash from the community if Elayne becomes more and more open.

Sometimes I get a little annoyed with Wayne when he decides to put on a dress just when we need to get someplace. I've got three kids to get ready and he's busy making himself pretty! Then, if I complain, instead of assisting he becomes a boss instead of a partner. I also get disgusted that he won't accept his male self—that he doesn't see its beauty or handsomeness.

Wayne, not Elayne, is my bed partner most of the time. He is gentle, though Elayne is even gentler. We both like to play the passive role. He prefers when I initiate and when I'm on top. He'll often wear a nightgown to bed. It's no big deal. I like the feeling of pantyhose in bed. It doesn't matter who wears them!

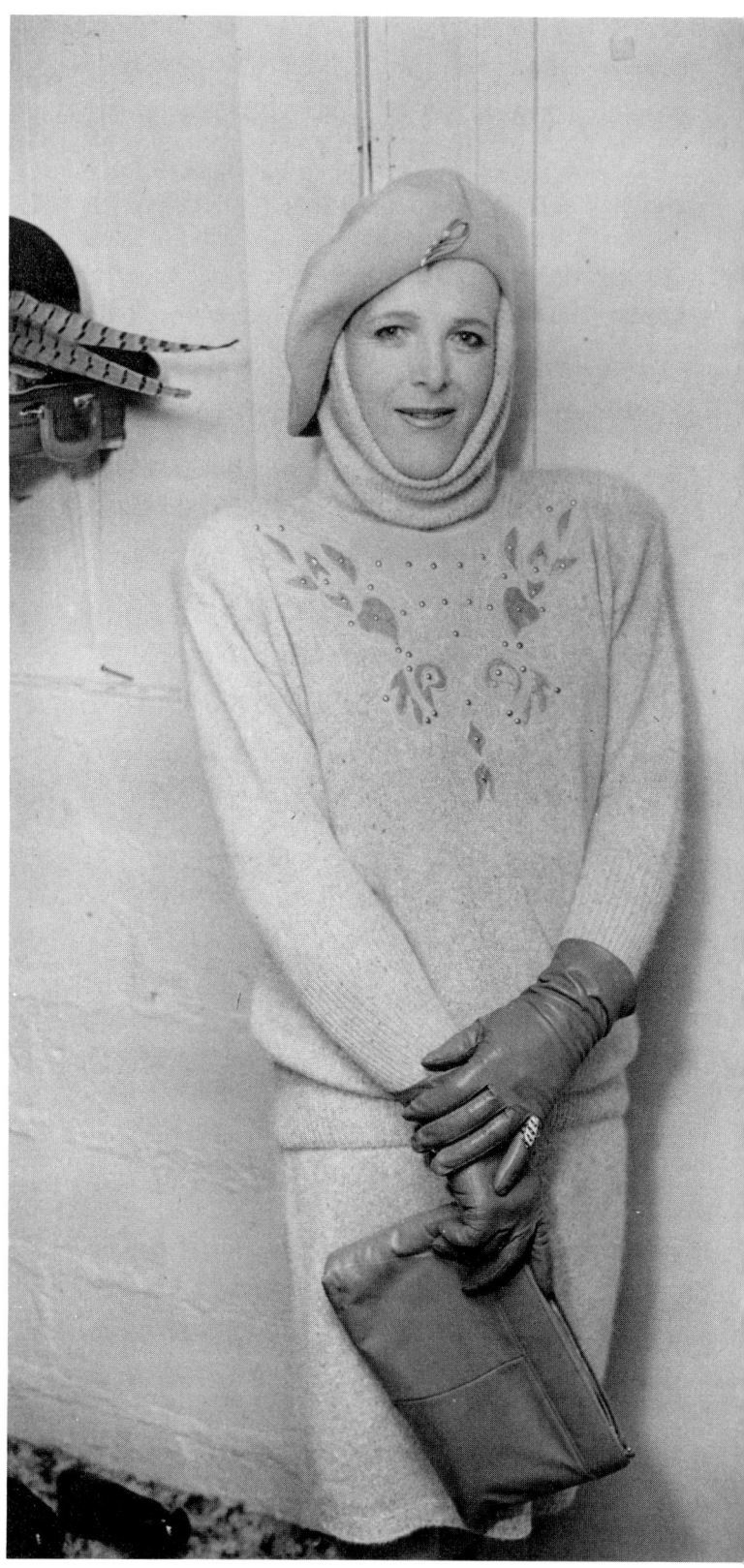

John, and John as Jennifer: "I could never go with a woman who wasn't fashionable."

JENNIFER

Because I was the oldest, I got all the beatings, nothing really bad, but my parents kept a whip. My father would hit me, but he was really a weakling. He tried to be a ladies' man. I never really liked him. I've always worn my hair long and he threatened that if I didn't cut it, he'd tie it up in ribbons.

The thing that attracted me to my wife is that she knew how to wear clothes. I could never go with a woman who wasn't fashionable. She never knew I was wearing her clothes when she went out. I was very paranoid about crossdressing, and any literature I had on it I used to hide because I was frightened that some burglar would come into the house and find it.

After a while, I wanted my wife to go out more and more, so I could wear her clothes, and I started withdrawing. I couldn't tell her what the problem was, so she asked for a divorce. We stayed friends, and she would often stop by after work. She popped in one time and there I was in the bathroom with her clothes on. It was an utter and complete shock to her. It wasn't until many years after that we started talking about it. Now, we are good friends.

The only sexual experience I've had has been with my wife, and I didn't like being the aggressor, being on top. I would have preferred being the woman. I don't like my penis. It doesn't seem like a part of me. I hide it between my legs all the time.

I really dislike men. The way they swagger around to show how tough they are, the crudeness. I've been with quite a few men when they've tried to pick up women, and it really upsets me, the tricks and lies they would say to women just to get in their pants. If I could be a woman, I'd be a businesswoman, and I'd be really hard on men. I'd have the advantage, because I know how men act, what turns them on. Not from what I've done, but from what I've seen other guys do to women.

ARIADNE

In the last fifteen to twenty years I emerged from being a closet crossdresser to being a leader in what I call the paraculture. This coming-out process has allowed me to pursue my identity as an androgyne. Androgynes are people who take elements of conventional masculinity and femininity and blend them in a way that is unique to their personal expression. They may use props like clothes, or they may use other kinds of symbolic imagery.

I'm a process-oriented person, and that's a very important distinction between me as an androgyne and people who are transgendered or crossdressers. They have goals: to look like Marilyn Monroe, or to really go through a serious transformation. My life is an odyssey. And my sense is that my odyssey will end when I leave this body and go to another world.

I was the firstborn male in my family, and in a Greek household that's a major event. Raised by five aunts, three uncles, and seventy-five cousins, I was cradled and given the most overwhelming love a child could ever get. Too much so. I didn't want all that fondling and all that caring.

I lived in New York, and never heard the term "transvestite" until I was about twenty-one, when I saw it in a bookstore. I was married to my first wife at the time, and didn't dream of going out in public, but I was interested in meeting other crossdressers.

In 1961 I made a friend in Boston. I was going through some real traumas and had to leave graduate school. He nurtured and succored me in many ways. He was not a crossdresser, but he appreciated my crossdressing and was fascinated after I came out to him. At that point, new windows opened up for me. I was living on my own. I told every woman that I went out with that I occasionally wore women's clothing. Much later I married again and we're very happy.

Ariadne: "Androgynes are people who take elements
of conventional masculinity and femininity and blend them
in a way that is unique to their personal expression."

Fashion show Fantasia Fair

In 1967 I saw an article about a person who had a club and helped people come out. I cut this article out and put it under the blotter on my desk. Every night I would read it like a Bible story and start to make the call and then hang up when someone answered. Finally, after eight months had elapsed, and with the help of a glass of ouzo, I screwed up enough courage to respond to the hello on the other end of the line. Another five months went by before I got up the mustard to go to a meeting. Guys came in wearing uniforms of all types: police uniforms, military uniforms, banker's suits, whatever! I went to the second floor of the duplex apartment and there were some very attractive women there. They were talking about football and baseball, or banking matters, and it would drift gradually to cosmetic things—"Where can you get wigs?" and so forth. These were the same people you'd meet in the street and never in a million years guess that they wore women's clothes.

That was the coming-out process. Within six months of that period I was catapulted into the position of being a leader and we founded a club called Cherrystone. That lasted for about six years before it metamorphosed into the Mayflower Club and, ultimately, the Tiffany Club. In 1975 we created Fantasia Fair, a yearly crossdresser gathering, and after the Fair, the Outreach Institute. It provides access to the gender community for helping professionals who may be looking at this phenomenon from a very skewed or narrow point of view.

In this culture we're expected to follow patterns of masculinity or femininity as they're prescribed. The problem is that human beings are not cut out that way because the culture has changed. I think the gender issue is basically a reaction to discontent with traditional gender roles. Workplaces where men have traditionally held forth have been challenged by women. Can a woman ever be a Green Beret? Damned right she could! Men have to look at this, and they are tortured by it. So we've seen the emergence of lots of men's groups. They're not necessarily saying, "Let's keep the status quo," but they are taking a good long look at their lives and a variety of alternatives. One of those happens to be a cross-gender mode.

I've talked to many crossdressers who look at life as a Walter Mitty-esque fantasy, only they're Jane Mitty! They imagine this incredible life of flowing boas and wonderful furs, and being wined and dined, and doors being opened—all of this Victoriana, which is what they think women are all about. They want to bring the inner and outer selves together but can't, because they have life patterns in which there's conflict: I can't go to my job dressed in a skirt, as much as I'd like to. If I do, I might lose my job. The man who loses his job loses his self-esteem, and its loss kills him.

My God! It is humanity that makes sense, not the clothes that anyone wears!

Maxine, Ariadne, and Virginia attending church service

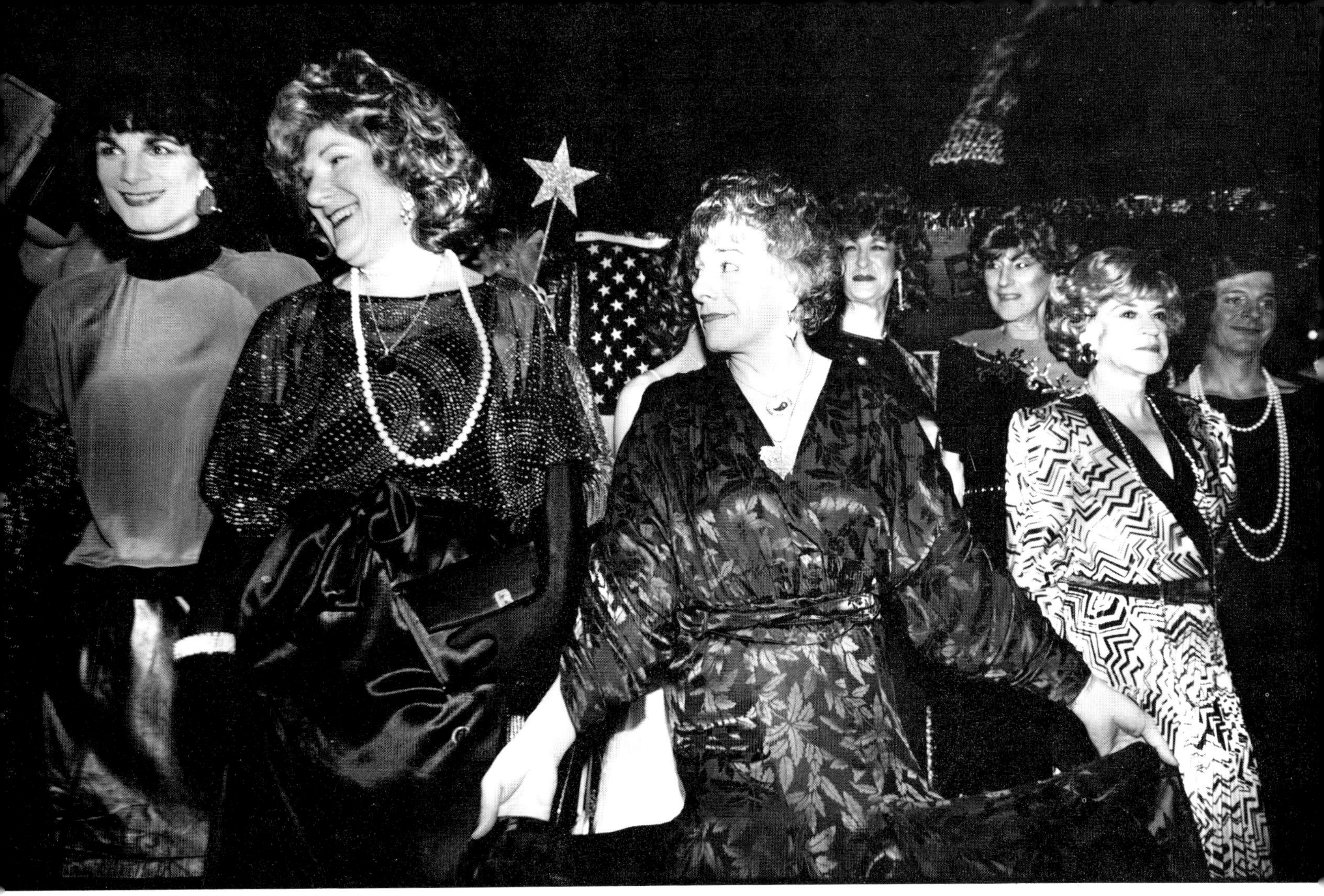

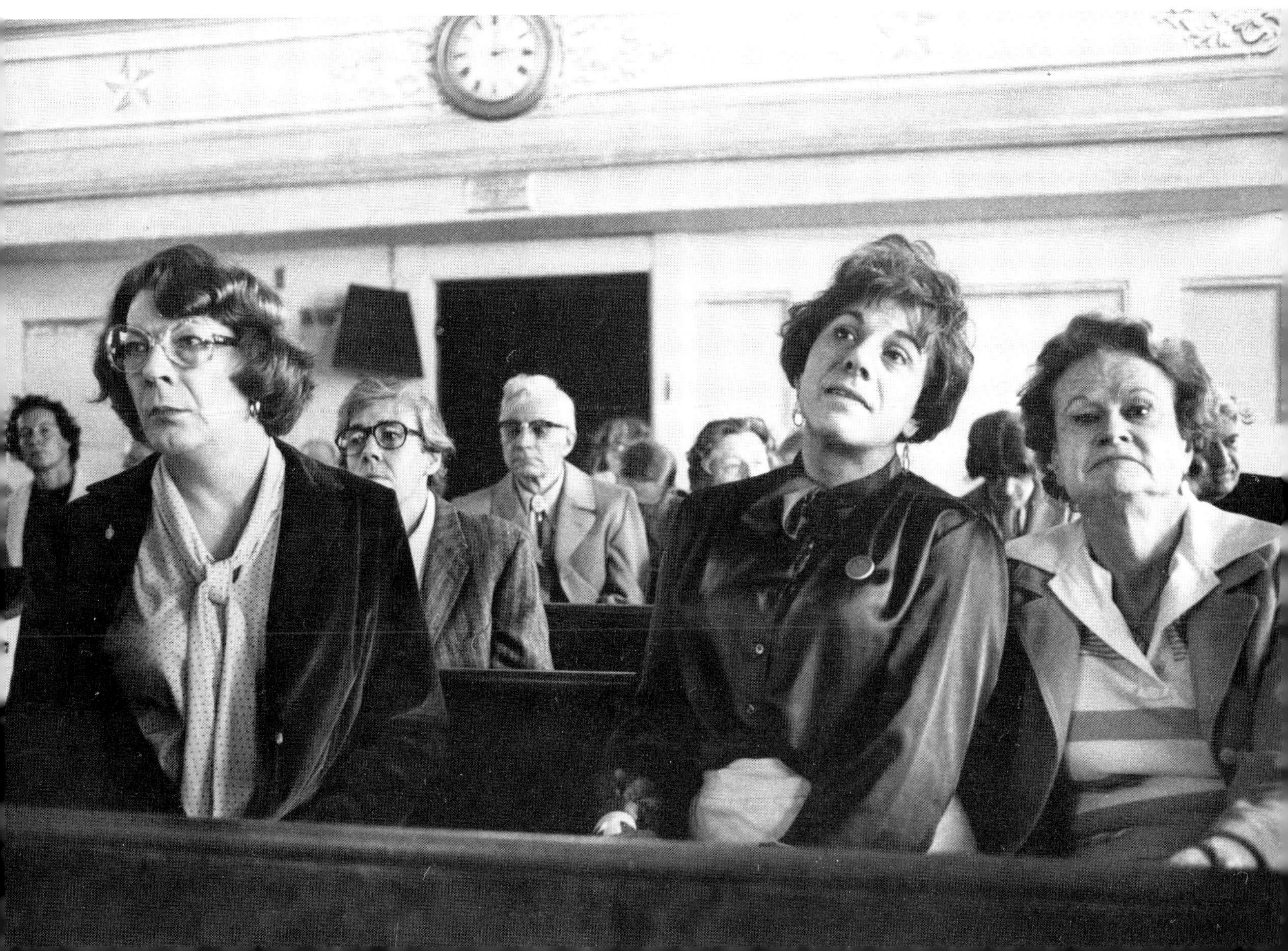

Amy and her husband, Rita.
Amy: "When somebody at the party asked me what I thought of him, I said, 'Ooh, I'm in love.'"

RITA

When I wear women's clothes, I feel sexy, calm, beautiful, healthy, sensual, vulnerable, graceful. I see more colors, more shades. My sexuality is more feminine; it includes more of my body. Suppressed feelings come to the surface. The liberation from suppression was the strongest feeling at first, even stronger than the feelings that went with the crossdressing itself. Men have feelings, but if we expressed them fully, they would be considered feminine. I had a normal upbringing, have a "normal" sexual orientation, experienced the usual negative reinforcement of behavior considered unsuitable for my gender. The "right" behavior was strongly reinforced by my parents, and especially by my peers.

When I want to feel sexy about my body, I don't always feel I can experience and express the full range in men's clothing. Men's clothing is functional. Women's clothes offset and reveal the body. A dress puts the legs on display.

I like to journey through the gender spectrum, from the masculine to the feminine, although I'll never get all the way to the end of the spectrum and really know what it's like to be a woman. Society influences me to be at either end of the spectrum, but is not comfortable with the middle range—it's a lot safer to look like a man or a woman. What I prefer is to be a guy being sexy and provocative. Androgynous clothing puts my male body on display. For the most part, people don't like androgyny, even at the Tiffany Club. Sometimes, when I go dressed the way I feel, I get a reaction like, "You call that crossdressing? What are you doing here?" I know that they're trying to integrate themselves into society, but I want to do that only some of the time.

I'm more self-critical when I want to pass as a woman. I'm trying hard to attain a brutally unattainable goal. When I'm in full regalia, wearing all the makeup, undergarments, wig, and high heels, I can't imagine how that could be sexual. That's untouchable, unapproachable, distancing. But being taken for a real woman is very exciting. You get treated differently. The whistling, the comments, the physical liberties. When I'm doing a stereotype, I get treated like a piece of ass by men and even by women.

TVism makes both men and women uncomfortable because it brings up the issue of homosexuality. I used to be homophobic, afraid to express the gay side of me. Then I realized that that was the feminine side of me and that I wasn't gay, I was a transvestite. It took me a long time to just enjoy looking at a transvestite. The first TV that I enjoyed looking at was myself. But it was a big step for me to just look up and down at another TV and really enjoy being with that person and see that TV as beautiful and sexy and feel OK about that. That was a lot of work for me.

When I'm getting dressed, it is almost like a form of meditation. It can be blissful. I can make a whole evening of it. Taking a bath, pampering, preening. The times I've really been satisfied with myself have had less to do with how I actually looked and more to do with my frame of mind. You are beautiful, period, and you become beautiful when you realize it. God made you that way, and people treat you that way when you realize it.

AMY (RITA'S WIFE)

Daniel and I met at a friend's party last year. I went into the kitchen to get some wine and saw this totally odd-looking person. Daniel had on a blue Frederick's of Hollywood pantsuit, blue high heels, a black hat, a yellow scarf, and a sequin belt. I thought he was quite beautiful. He was very tall, obviously bold, or artistic, or crazy! I was taken in and stunned. I couldn't even start a conversation. When somebody at the party asked me what I thought of him, I said, "Ooh, I'm in love!"

My initial attraction was to an original, artistic creation, whereas the TVism I've been exposed to since then—where men want to pass as women and want to camouflage their maleness and do all this artificial stuff to create a woman's figure—that's not as artistic or creative, that's a charade. I'm not attracted to men portraying women. Daniel has millions of images. He always produces something that feels true to where he is at the time. Most of the TVs I've met have a certain person they turn into that looks like their mother.

Having him get dressed up and go out to pass as a woman, and getting into that untouchable state, is unpleasant to me. I would rather be able to be physical with my partner no matter what he's wearing. Crossdressing is a solitary practice, an internal state. It's distancing. It's not something that involves a partner, although we can play with it together sometimes.

Being able to create these feminine images himself has liberated Daniel from being caught up in the image of women. I really appreciate having a partner who is aware of the images women create, because men in our culture will often see a woman totally made up and think that's natural. It's very difficult to look as good as Daniel when he gets dressed up. It's irritating to go to parties and have Daniel be the prettiest thing at the party. He's a real peacock! Having grown up as a woman in this culture, I've learned ways of deflecting the energy that produces the kind of attention I didn't want to receive. So, having gotten so perfect at that, I met Daniel and he ruined the whole thing!

VALERIE

I grew up on welfare. My father had tuberculosis and couldn't work. I met him for the first time when I was three or four when he came home from one of his hospital stays. Even though he lived with us, my father was not allowed to touch any of us because he was considered contagious. He showed me affection by teaching me how to make things and how to use tools. My sister, who is four years older than me, and her friend played family, and I was the little girl. I don't recall whose idea it was.

    It wasn't until two years ago that Valerie began to emerge publicly. I went to see *The Rocky Horror Picture Show* and was fascinated to see how the people responded. Something started ticking there. Then I saw some sexy things in a store and decided to wear them to a Halloween party. A window had opened.

    I live near a nightclub that features female impersonators, and it was around this time that my wife suggested we go to one of the shows. After that, I began going to the club "dressed." Eventually, news about my appearance at the club leaked to my wife's family and she thought she might want a divorce. We went to a psychologist and pretty soon he realized that he wasn't getting anywhere, so he called the Gay and Lesbian Hotline and they referred me to Ariadne Kane.

    I really don't have much interest in passing publicly as a woman. I would prefer to have people know that I am a man in women's clothing. I would like to be accepted for who I am, not what I do, or how much money I make or even for how I look. As Henry, people are a little afraid of me. As Henry, I jump if a man touches me. I can't stand it. That's what society has taught me. But when I'm dressed as Valerie I feel good about the affection and warmth I feel when someone *like me* touches me. It feels natural.

    One Halloween, my son Eric decided to attend a costume party dressed as a girl. He insisted on using his own allowance to pay for the clothes and shoes, and asked me to drive him to the store. By paying for the costume himself, he avoided making me feel responsible. I was very moved by this, and felt much closer to him, but I also felt some sadness and realized that I'd been less affectionate to Eric than I had to his sister, Kimberly.

On New Year's Eve I invited my wife, Betsy, and a friend, Louis, to a gay bar. I wore a short, strapless black lace dress—size seven!—a long blond wig and lots of makeup. I felt very sexy that night. I wanted to dance with Louis, but he wouldn't go that far. To me, it seemed innocent enough, but I guess it really wasn't. Betsy wouldn't dance with me either. Three other crossdressers I knew were there, so I danced with them. Betsy's experience at the bar that night tipped the scale. She said it confirmed all her suspicions. She was ready to see a lawyer.

Eric, Valerie, and Kimberly at the mall

Eric, his father, Valerie, and sister Kimberly

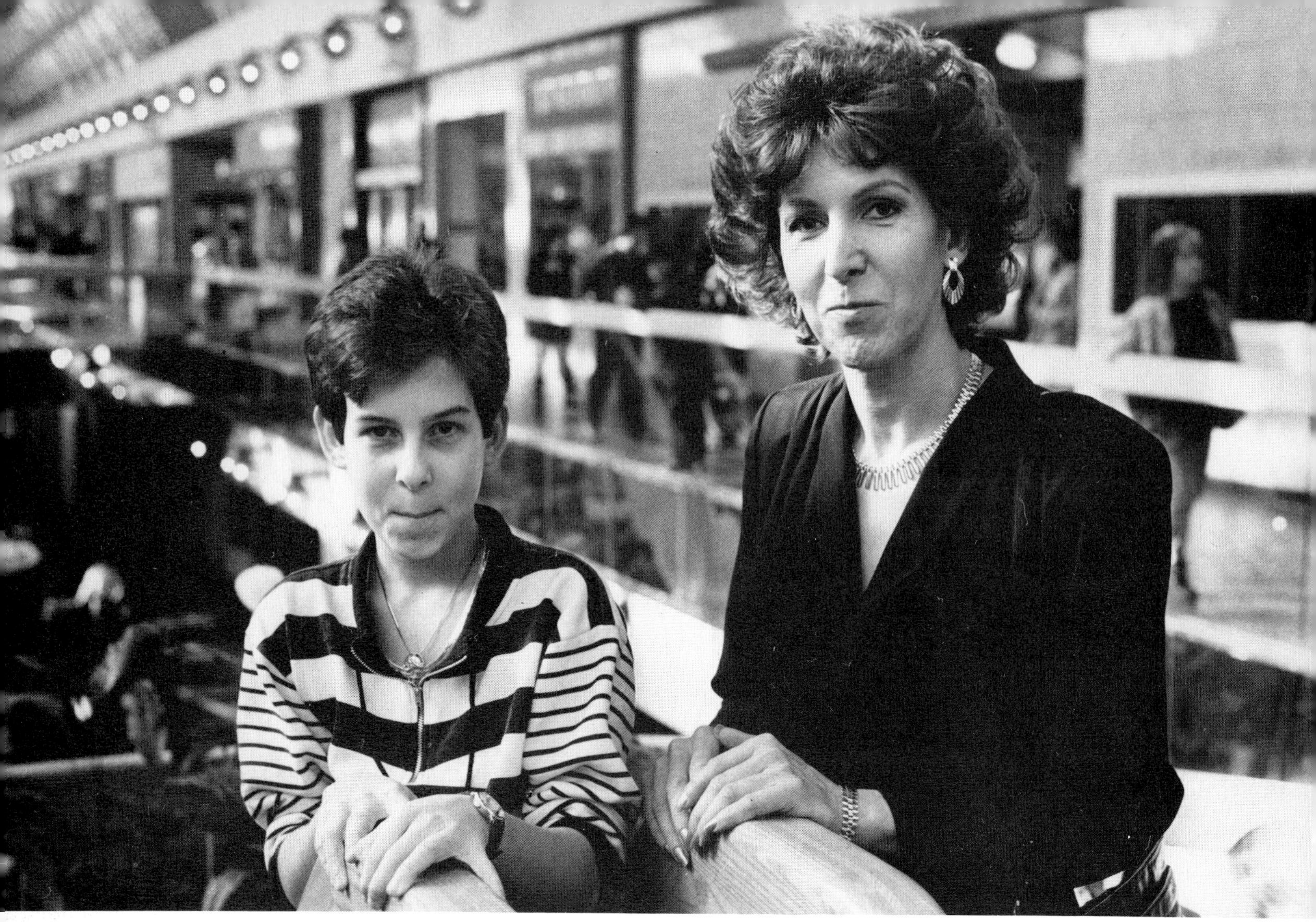

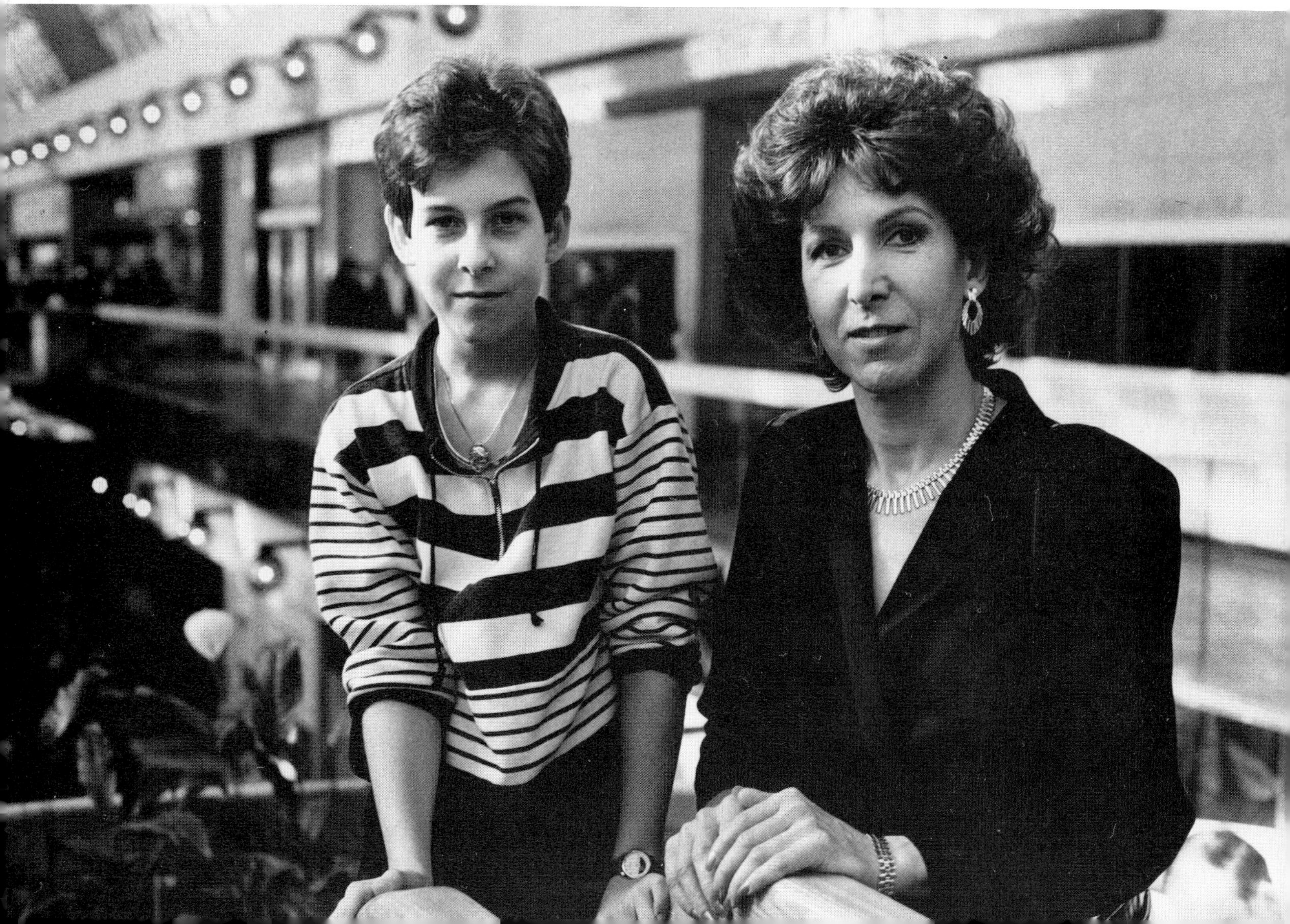

Eric and Valerie

Eric and Kimberly watch their father put on makeup

Eric and Valerie

Valerie in the park

ALLISON

Once, while my grandparents were caring for me they took me to the doctor, and since I didn't cry during the visit, my grandfather said I could have any toy I wanted. We went to the toy store and I picked out a great big doll. What he didn't know was that I took the doll back to my room, and after everyone had gone away, I crawled under the bed and tried to put on the doll's clothes, but they were too small. I remember crying under the bed.

I grew up in Oklahoma, and my parents were very well off, although my father lost his money during World War II through a combination of drinking, gambling, and bad business investments. I have photographs of neighbor girls who would baby-sit and dress me in girls' clothes. When I was twelve my father caught me wearing my mother's pedal pushers, a blouse, a halter, and a scarf around my head, and I had on a pair of her wedgies. He just grinned and said, "Don't you look silly." I was so embarrassed. He didn't tell me to take it off, I just did. I started maturing, and realized this was affecting me in a sexual way.

Sometimes I'd get dressed and look in the mirror, and the way the mirror and the sink were, I could just . . . basically I was making love to the sink. Then I would relieve myself in the sink without knowing what was going on. I'd just received an admonishment at my confirmation class about "not spilling your seed upon the rocks," and of course it was an abomination for men to put on women's clothes or do anything effeminate. I remember fighting that, and I went to bed praying that I would never do this. I woke up the next morning and I had stockings on, held up by adhesive tape. I didn't remember doing it!

Something was happening in my life, and it was through hypnosis that I'm able to recall a lot of this. I learned that if I wasn't aware of these actions, then another self inside of me had done something to relieve these urges. From the age of twelve until recently, there was a totally different and distinct personality who did these things!

At that time "it" had no name. I just did things with no conscious memory of them. I went away to college swearing I wasn't going to lose control again. Well, no sooner did I get to school than I went to my mailbox and found a C.O.D. package from Sears that contained an all-in-one brief and a slip! I would order things without realizing it.

One night I came to, you might say, at the end of a movie wearing stockings, a cheap little skirt, a sweater, a babushka, and snow boots. Fortunately, I recognized what theater it was, and was able to make my way back home. Even though there was another personality, my conscious self as Al still wanted to dress. It never relieved my own desire. That's very aggravating, isn't it?

I met Patsy and fell head over heels in love with her. She fulfilled every ideal I had, so I purged. I said, "This time, I'm not going to let the other person come." And I went almost eight months.

"Missy Allison" at an abandoned steel mill:
"I imagined what it must have been like working in a dirty grimy job.
What if one of them was a TV?"

Halloween was coming up, and I told Patsy that I'd always had the urge to dress like a woman for Halloween and hadn't. Wouldn't it be fun? I thought that I'd do it just once under *my* terms. She dressed like a Russian general, and I went as a Russian peasant woman with a big babushka and boots. We were sitting in the backseat of a car waiting for her brother to come out, and suddenly I couldn't fight it, the other person came! Patsy said she thought I had gone into some kind of stupor or trance. I hadn't had a drink. I was afraid that the other personality might come out if I drank. It turned out that this kind of multiple personality is considered an auto-self-hypnotic state. Basically, it was a relaxation response. If I really relaxed, that person could be made to come.

When I told Patsy about it she said, "Well, we're going to cure this thing." So we started doing research. Obviously, this person, whom we named Linda, wanted to be real. It was very interesting, because Linda started writing notes to Patsy, but it was the scrawl of a child. Linda was left-handed. I'm not, but as a child I might have been. Linda was Catholic, and I'm hard-shelled Protestant. Linda would try to smoke, I will *never* smoke. Linda tried to create a totally opposite personality. Basically, that's what Patsy lived with for twenty-one years.

Allison

I went through a mid-life crisis, and what was thought to be a heart attack. After many Valium prescriptions and visits to emergency wards a doctor finally said, "I think you'd better see a psychiatrist." I said, "Who? *Me?*" But I knew I really had to.

Once there, it took only thirty minutes before the psychiatrist said, "You're not telling me the real problem." Finally I said, "I think I'm either a transsexual or a transvestite. To make matters worse, I have at least one other personality." He said, "What!" He'd never dealt with a multiple personality. For the next five years we worked through a lot of things, peeling back the apple. We dealt with family relations, my dominating mother, all the different issues, but he kept putting off dealing with the central core.

Linda got better and better, because she now became not a closet transvestite, but a basement transvestite, working with Patsy on her artistic projects. They became good friends and worked from ten P.M. to two A.M. Oddly enough, it never affected my work the next day. I went to work just as fresh as if I'd slept all night! I needed less sleep as two personalities than I do as one.

My psychiatrist's idea of merging the personalities was to have me get dressed and encourage Linda to come without losing consciousness. That was the weirdest thing. When I saw something that Linda made I'd recognize it, but I wouldn't recall doing it. I might remember Patsy and Linda had blueberry pie and tea that night. If I saw a movie as Linda, and then again as Al, I'd have only vague recollections of having seen certain scenes before. Linda could buy me a Christmas present and I would remember nothing. I'd be totally surprised!

My corporation transferred me to another region, and by good fortune I rented an apartment that the previous tenant had decorated in a very feminine manner. In that apartment I was able to work very hard at integrating the personalities. I kept a diary, and it was during that time that I named myself. "We" took the Al and Linda and made Alinda, then all of a sudden the name Allison hit me.

The psychiatrist finally admitted that he couldn't help me with Linda, so he put me in touch with a gender counseling clinic. And in just an hour, I came to the conclusion that Linda's days were numbered. I took a whole battery of tests, and the psychologist told me that I scored very high as far as being a possible transsexual, but then he said, "You haven't said the magic words yet. You've never said that you wanted to be a woman. You only want to appear as a woman. You'd be using a change of sex simply as a license to crossdress, and we can give you that license *without* surgery."

To the best of my knowledge, that was the beginning of the end for Linda. I realized that Linda existed only because Al could not bear the guilt of dressing up in women's clothing. She was my escape mechanism. Now, I can allow the feminine part of me to express itself through Allison, without the guilt, and with the added advantage of remembering every delicious moment.

This year Patsy put on a Christmas party for Allison. I can't even talk about it now without choking up. A Christmas stocking with nail polish and perfume, bubble bath, and beautiful skirts, blouses, and pajamas. It was just a magnificent party. She said, "I just want you to know how much I really accept you."

EVE

There is one date in my life that symbolizes Eve's need for existence more than any other—January 24, 1945. Influenced by Goebbels's propaganda and my own involvement in the Hitler Youth, we felt very secure living in Marienburg, in eastern Germany. It was, therefore, a complete surprise to us when, on that day, grenades began to destroy some of the buildings near us, and eventually took out part of the apartment in which we lived. My father, an officer in the German army, was fighting the Russian army, and except for leave to recuperate from one of his thirteen war wounds, had not been home since Hitler declared war on Poland in 1939.

In the panic that followed, Mother took charge, ordering all of us, my brother, fourteen, my sister, seven, and myself, twelve, to pack our most important belongings into knapsacks, and we took to the street. Our flight away from the oncoming Russians was slow, especially since my grandmother, who had been staying with us, found it difficult to trudge through the snow. At nightfall we found refuge in a barn. The next morning brought two disturbing discoveries. Grandmother had died of exhaustion and the bitter cold, and, when my mother examined our knapsacks, she found, to her utter surprise, that I had packed a blouse and a skirt, symbolic of my favorite possessions. To my dismay, she threw them away, ignoring my tearful expression, and dismissing it as a lark. The need to express my femininity had developed at the age of seven. That blouse and skirt had been my secret wardrobe. I just felt they were more suited to me than the boy's things I got to wear.

Even though, in the years that followed, my interest in anything feminine continued to persist, my instinct told me that having been born a boy, I'd better pursue that role. All my energy went into the development of my athletic ability, progressing from a small town soccer team to a professional first division team and, ultimately, to the German National squad.

Germany was still economically deprived in those days, and the occasional Hollywood movie portrayed an altogether unfamiliar world of luxury, inhabited by beautiful actresses wearing beautiful clothes and makeup. So, with sixty-four dollars in our pockets, my wife and I arrived in the United States. I was still very much an island in terms of my knowledge of what made me want to behave like a woman. Then, one day, I saw the headlines about Christine Jorgensen. Influenced by Christine's story, I blurted out my secret desires to my wife, insisting that she see me all decked out. Instead of acceptance, this led to her wanting a divorce, a wish that lingered and permeated our marriage for eighteen years until it finally happened.

Eve—an Industrialist

In 1962 my lonesome world suddenly came to an end. I came across an article in *Sexology* magazine written by Virginia Prince reporting on a survey of "166 Men in Dresses." Contacts were made, and the determination for Eve's right to exist became ever stronger. Out of all this has come the happy ending like the Hollywood I envied. I met a woman who fell in love with me at precisely the same instant I did with her. As she puts it, she saw the person beneath that pretty dress. Eve is there every day. On some days, she will put on her male drag and cheerfully earn a comfortable living for the three of us. I have found a marvelous partner and peace of mind. *I love life!*

Eve: "Eve is there every day. On some days, she will put on her male drag and cheerfully earn a comfortable living."

PAULA

I was an only child, spoiled by my parents and grandparents. My grandmother would always say, "I wish we had a little girl," although they never treated me like a little girl. One day when my mother and I were visiting my grandparents, I found a bracelet and a blouse and put them on, and they said, "Oh look! There's our little girl." It became a game. My mother would let me crossdress when I couldn't go out to play. We had two neighborhood girls who were my age, and a couple of times we played dress-up together. I stopped dressing for a few years until puberty. At that time I learned about masturbation, and it became a fetish. All the feelings I didn't have for girls, and all the feelings I did have for boys, I thought were related to crossdressing.

As a teenager, I remember wearing my mother's skirt and blouse, and taking some pictures of myself in them. When I went away to the university, my father cleaned out my room and found them. One day when I was home, he called me out to the garage and said, "I found these pictures and I thought you might like to keep them." I remember being told about my father's escapades on Halloween. He used to go out in drag; you could say that he introduced camp to our small Michigan town.

At the university, I lived in a dormitory and couldn't crossdress, so I would fantasize about it during masturbation. I met Judy, and we had a very good relationship. After about a year and a half of dating, we started to have sex. I told her that I crossdressed because I didn't have a sexual outlet except for that fetish. I didn't feel guilty about crossdressing per se, but I felt guilty about substituting regular, heterosexual sex with this fantasy. I felt more guilt about the masturbating than the crossdressing. For the first couple of years after Judy and I were married, I had no desire to crossdress. Gradually, I began to masturbate and fantasize more and more. I went out and bought makeup. I liked the feel of lipstick. I tried Judy's clothes on. She eventually accepted my crossdressing to a degree; I could introduce some bit of crossdressing in our lovemaking.

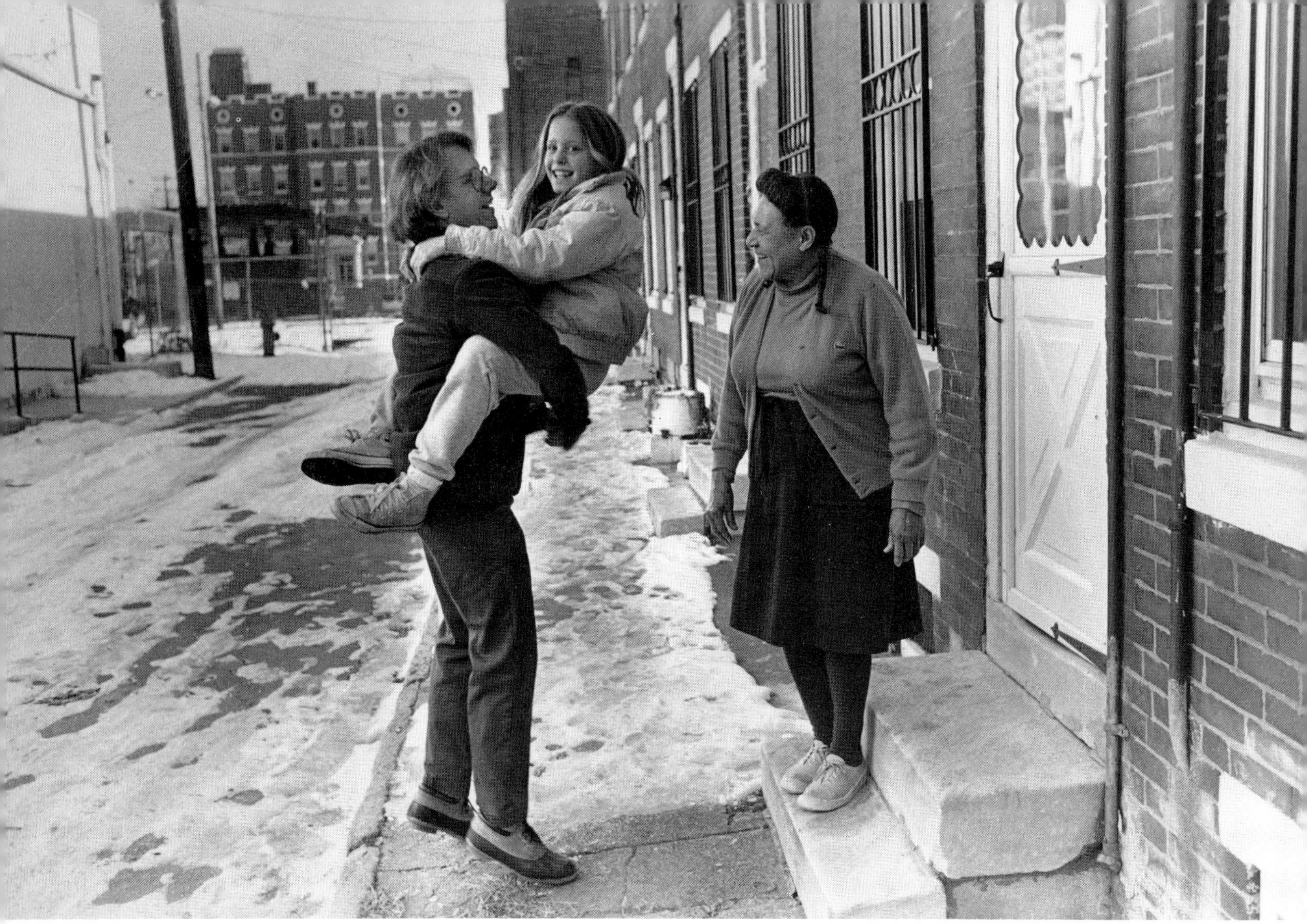

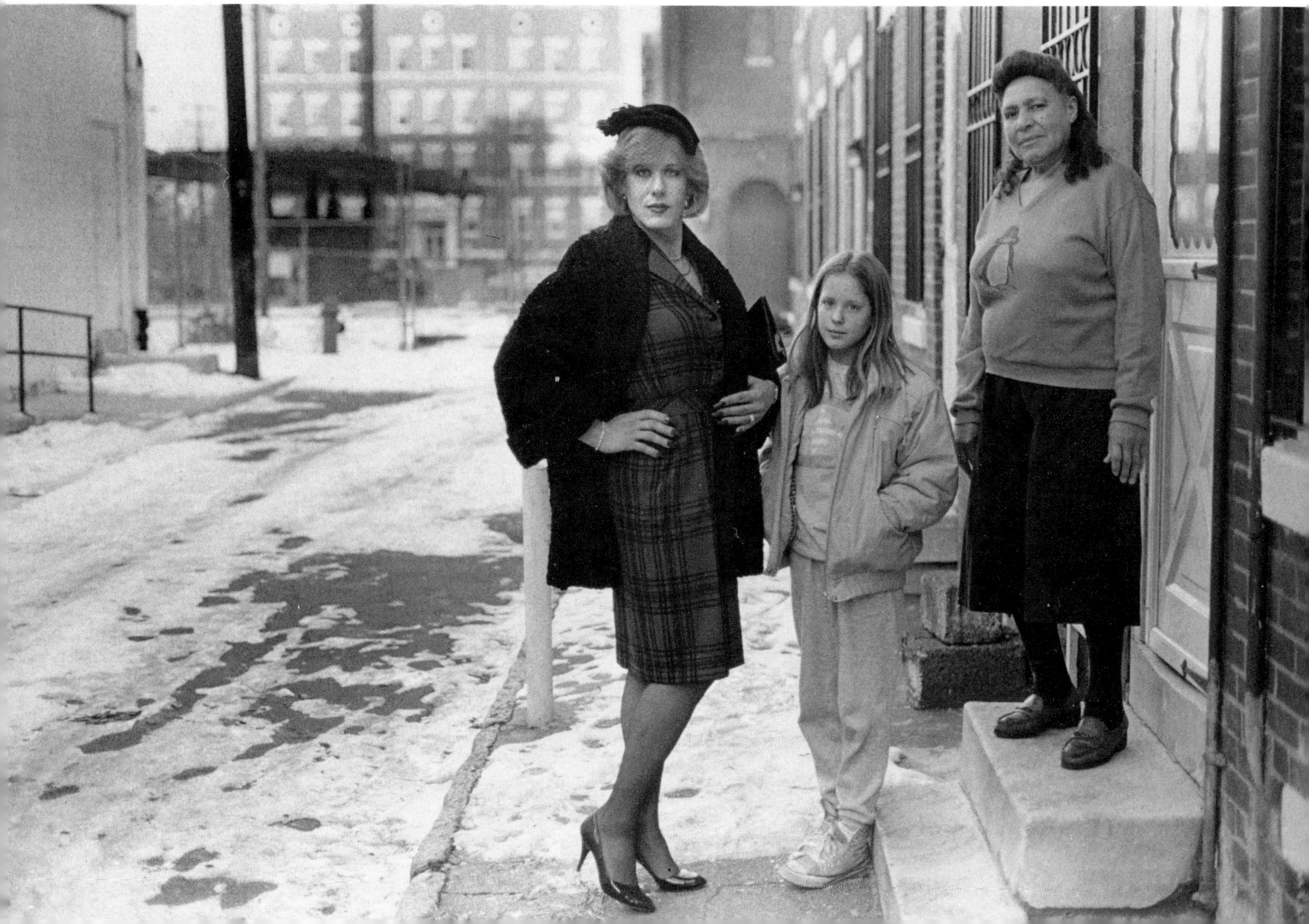

Paul with daughter Lisa and neighbor

Judy and I became parents. It was the best thing that could have happened to me. We were thinking of joining the Mormon church and were told we should have children. We moved to Washington, where I was stationed at the Pentagon as a public affairs officer for the Navy. I discovered I was gay when I was twenty-nine, after our daughter was born. Judy was angry and upset, but after a while she accepted it. I reassured her that I loved her, and we still made love. If I was seeing a man I didn't crossdress because gay men don't like crossdressing. If they wanted a woman, they would be with one. I couldn't say, "I do drag, that's why I shave my legs." It was very difficult integrating the sex and the crossdressing. Judy and I finally separated, not because of the crossdressing, but because she feared that

Paula and daughter Lisa playing dress-up

Paul as Paula with daughter Lisa and neighbor

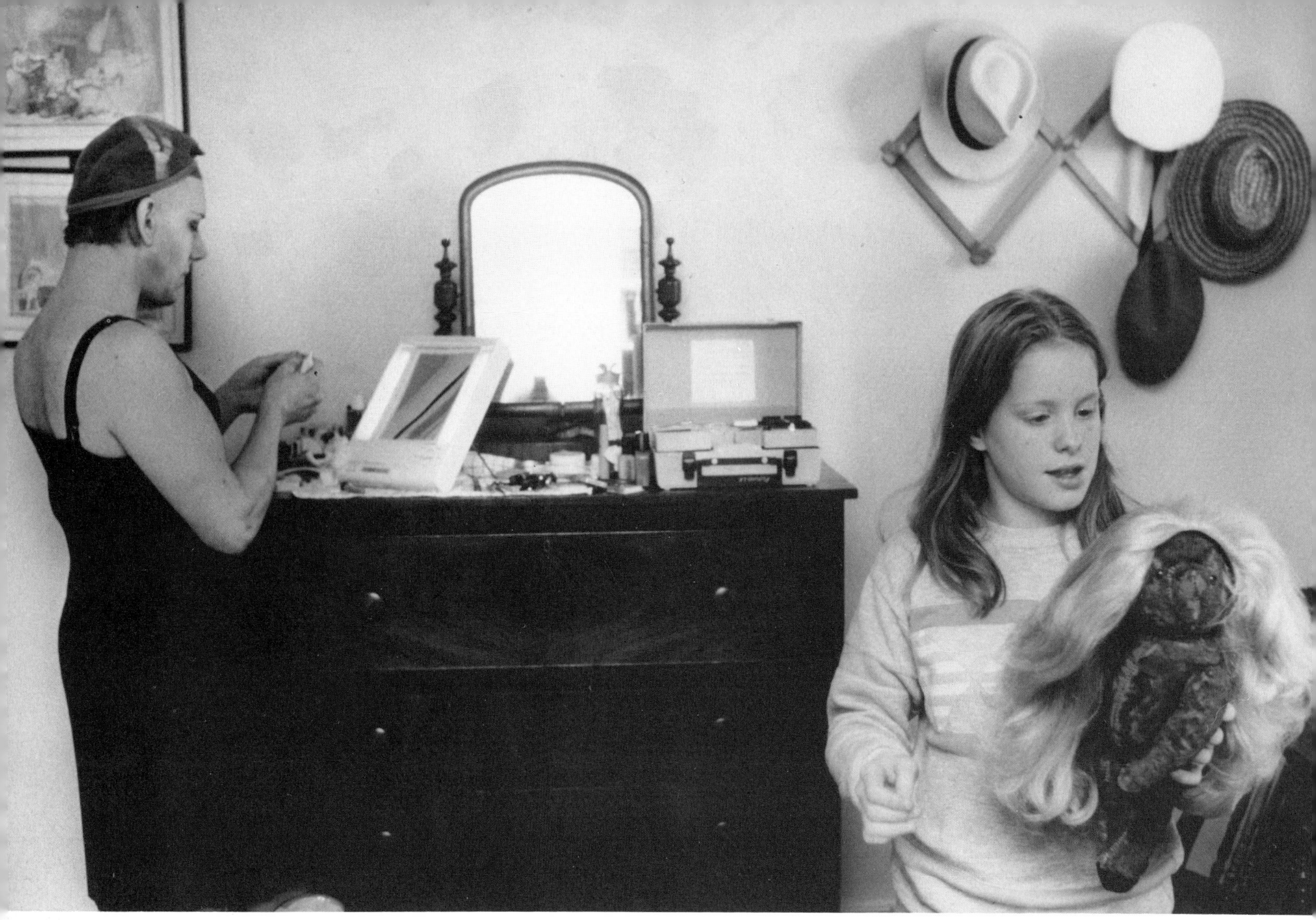

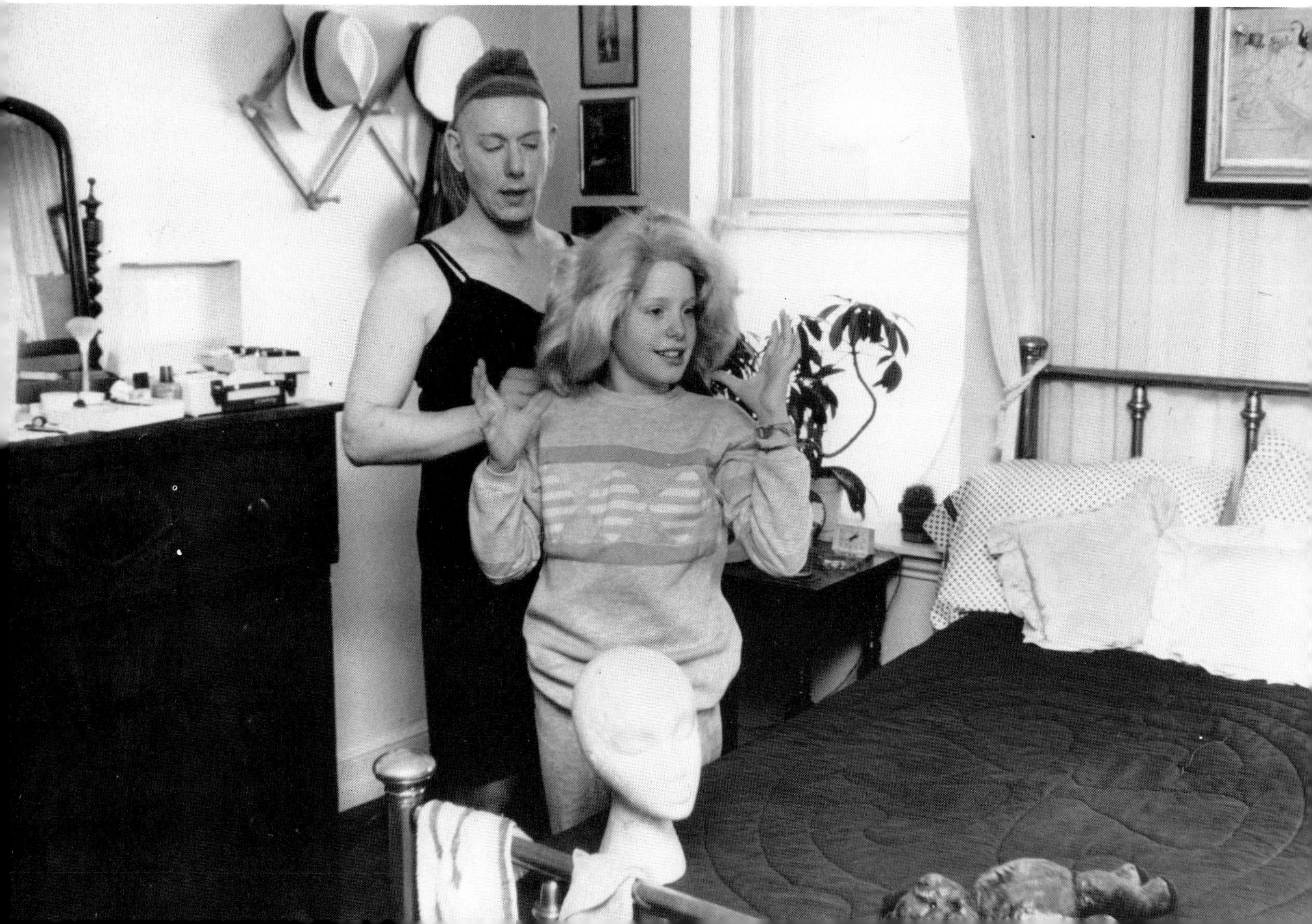

one day I would meet Mr. Right and leave her. After going through a difficult period of trying to meet men and needing to crossdress, I finally decided that some guy I meet may be gone in two weeks, but crossdressing is going to be with me forever!

I ended up joining an Anglican church, where the priests and deacons are in high drag. I've always been religious, a true desire from inside, not because I feel like a nasty person because I crossdress or am attracted to men. I'll go out on a Saturday night as Paula, and be too tired to undress before bed, so I'll kneel beside the bed and pray, with my fake nails, my lipstick, and my earrings on. I don't feel there is anything insulting about that.

I started to get into crossdressing in a serious way. I became adept. I came to realize that what I do is art. Paula Sinclair is a character that I've created. It's an outlet for the personality that's Paul Grayson. For me it's not a question of masculine/feminine, it's just a role. When I'm Paula, I keep my knees together, I don't schlump down the street, I always wear heels because they fit the character. When I'm done, it feels good to get out of the heels and scratch my head and rub my face.

I was asked to resign from the Navy because of my homosexuality and I went to work in media relations for another branch of government in Philadelphia. I became politically active in both the gay and the crossdressing communities. I've been on television shows, and everyone at work knows about my lifestyle and seems to accept it. My neighbors accept me, too. It is always a special experience to have older ladies who live on my street come up to me and tell me how pretty I look, or to have men in the neighborhood wave at me when I'm dressed, and speak to me as a man when I'm not.

I believed that I didn't need to tell Lisa, my daughter, about my crossdressing, not because she wouldn't understand, but because I didn't want to burden her with my secret. But she was picking up clues, so I decided that unless I wanted to lie to her and make up stories about the high heels under my bed, or my shaved arms and legs, I had to explain. I assured her that I've been a transvestite since before she was born. The only difference was that now she would know something about me that she didn't know before. Shortly after I told her, we went out for dinner with a transvestite friend and his daughter. Both of us fathers were in drag, and the girls were very relaxed. When Lisa and I got back to my house, I explained that I had wanted her to meet JoAnn and Anna so she wouldn't feel like she had the only father in the world who liked to wear a dress. I believe that telling her has brought us closer together, for she sees that there are no secrets between us. I may not be a typical father, but she shows me that she loves me because I am *her* father.

suzy

I'm thirty-two, the third of four boys, and I've been crossdressing since I was twelve or thirteen. I've been fairly comfortable with it all my life, but I realized it wasn't something that people were going to be very open or accepting of, so I was in the closet until I was twenty-six, when I saw an ad for a weekend for transvestites. I went, and it changed my life. At that time, the only person who knew about Suzy was my therapist. After the weekend, I wanted to tell the whole world. I haven't lost any friends over it yet. I feel like a new person since I came out.

My mother was a tomboy, so there was something mystical about not having someone feminine in the family. There is evidence that all four of us boys crossdressed. I remember one of my brothers was caught crossdressing once. We came home and he was standing in a girdle and bra, looking in a mirror. One time, when we were ridiculing him about it, my dad said, "Don't do that. All boys do that, I did it when I was a kid, too." My father is a very good man. I have a very good relationship with my parents.

At the time I discovered crossdressing, I also discovered masturbation. I liked the feel of the clothes. It wasn't until later that I realized there was more I could do with this. I never thought I could look good.

I was a virgin until I was twenty-six. It wasn't until after I came out that I had a sexual experience. It's still a part of my sexual excitement. Mary and I have a pretty good sex life, but my fantasies about this are still an active part of it. She helps out with it, too. She'll create plots, fantasies with me.

MARY (SUZY'S GIRLFRIEND)

I'm twenty-one, a student at a small Catholic college outside of Chicago. Suzy is one of my professors. I'd been attracted to him for a while. There was a gentle side to him that I wanted to get to know. We began to realize there was more than a student-teacher involvement. I invited him to a Halloween party. I showed up as Mickey Mouse, and he showed up as a cheerleader! He'd shaved his legs—the whole bit—and I thought, This guy's got guts to come out in front of the students. The next week we got together, and after hours of talking he said, "Suzy wasn't just a character, it's part of me." At first I was in

Mary and Pete as Suzy. Mary: "I invited him to a Halloween party, I showed up as Mickey Mouse, and he showed up as a cheerleader!"

shock, but I decided I care about him as a man, I care about her as a woman. Now I think both of us are changing in our femme roles. I've decided to make myself more feminine, since I found out about Suzy. I've always been a tomboy, but you wouldn't know that, seeing me now.

Suzy took me to a meeting of the Chicago Gender Society. I met all these people and thought, These are women. When I see them dressed as men, I don't know how to approach them because I'm used to thinking of them as my good girlfriends. When I start bitching and moaning about the cost of pantyhose, they know, they've been there. One of them's a Tupperware lady. There was a crossdressing convention that I went to recently, and, forgetting that these are really men, I started to change in front of them!

Mary and boyfriend, Pete, a professor

*Dan and Yvonne. Dan: "We have reversed roles.
A genetic female, I am the aggressor, the protector. I find myself worrying that
I will take advantage of Yvonne."*

YVONNE AND DAN

YVONNE

Today my name is Yvonne. Yesterday my name was George. Yesterday was a long time ago. Today I live completely as a woman.

George fathered three children and is a grandparent of two. In my past, I tried to achieve, in every way, what other people thought I should achieve to be successful. Owning my own business and other material things were nice by other people's standards.

Yvonne has emerged into a lifestyle that is caring, sharing, and making other people happy . . . hurting no one. My life has become successful by just being me. My day is worth every minute, because I'm happy with myself and those around me.

After having been alone within myself, now I have the rare opportunity of being challenged by a relationship with a crossdresser. Daniel is a female-to-male crossdresser. Sometimes I get more confused doing the laundry than I think anyone in the world could possibly get! The fun thing is watching who the waitress gives the check to, me or Dan. How important it is, that lovemaking is more than just a simple orgasm. It's finding time to hold, to hug, and feel close to and within the shelter and security that love brings. Dan and Yvonne's life is based on helping people find for themselves that tomorrow is going to be a great day.

DAN

Yvonne and I have known each other for a year and a half. However, it's been only since September that we've begun our journey as lovers and best friends, with a mutual concern and compassion for the crossdressing and transsexual community.

The fourth child in a family of two boys and four girls, I grew up with mixed views and values regarding my femininity. On the one hand, I loved and copied both my mother and my older sister, getting into their makeup and nail polish, et cetera. On the other hand, I spent a fair amount of time playing in the dirt, climbing farm tractors and trees with an older brother, playing cowboys and Indians, and kick-the-can.

I was wearing my brother's clothes by age seven and had kissed my best girlfriend by age ten. During my growing-up years, no comments were made about my favoring my brother's shirts over my own. No one chastised me, or confronted me on any related issue with the exception of the "fact" that girls don't kiss their girlfriends on the lips.

As an inquisitive scientist, I loved nature, plants, farming, and people, often reading autobiographies. I became a loner, an eccentric, preferring solitude or investigation to social situations with my peers.

It was not until I was confronted with my crossdressing that I began to fully explore and understand who I am and where this crossdressing fits in—why I have felt so uncomfortable in feminine dress and naturally comfortable in masculine dress, both in masculinized women's business suits and masculine dress itself. This comfort in crossdressing is not a purely physical comfort, it is also emotional and psychological. It is the comfort of congruity of feelings, thoughts, and expression. I feel more confident making my own decisions when I am freed up inside mentally and emotionally to respond in a direct manner, as Dan. I am considerate of others, yet I am able to see more options, and I am better able to take good care of myself.

My relationship with Yvonne is very special. I find I'm accepting myself for the first time, because I am acting the way I feel inside and not being critical of myself, or comparing myself to my sisters or female peers who have chosen a more standard lifestyle. In many ways, our lifestyle is very similar to that of the average male and female lovers' relationship. The difference being that we have reversed roles. A genetic female, I am the aggressor, the protector, the initiator. I find myself worrying that I will take advantage of her, to get my own way. It is a strange and wonderful adventure for us both as we learn to trust our feelings, and share our intimate needs with each other.

DIAHANNA

Eight years ago, I decided to go out as Diahanna for the first time. As I was driving along my little Bug blew a tire. I pulled to the side and just stood there, shocked that I'd have to change the tire in heels, stockings, and a skirt. The California Highway Patrol came driving up with the red flashing lights. The blood was rushing to my head and I thought, I'm gonna get arrested! The guy came up and said, "I'll give you a hand," and he did! He then zipped off into the darkness.

My grandmother kept her lipsticks on top of an antique bureau that was like a seashell. I was around four when I tried the lipstick and got it all over me. I got a spanking for that. My grandfather said, "Little boys don't play with girls' things." I remember there was this lady named Ruthie, and she was a very sensuous woman. She had a shape that would put a Coca-Cola bottle to shame! I remember her saying to my mother, "You know, Joey is so cute, he shoulda been a girl."

At age eleven, I was heavy into masturbation, and I really got off on my female mirror image. I used tennis balls for breasts, and black synthetic rope that I uncorded and combed out as my wig. I think I wanted to be another Ruthie. At the time, I was real good with a yo-yo. One day a yo-yo popped back to me, hit me on my breast, and it swelled up. I got a thrill by wondering, How can I do it to the other side?

When I was thirteen, my parents split up. My father was into gadgetry and fixing things. I think I got the basics of being a man from him. He was there, but I could never confide in him.

When I went public about my crossdressing and appeared on television, I finally told my father. He said, "It's your life. You can do what you want, I don't think any less of you. You're still my son and I love you." That was perhaps the first time I ever heard my dad say he loved me. It was beautiful. I felt a tremendous pressure suddenly vanish.

I got involved with experimental theater while I attended Berkeley. I was in a minstrel show, where the black man was made up in whiteface, and the white man was made up in blackface. I got the opportunity to act the white woman. That got me wanting

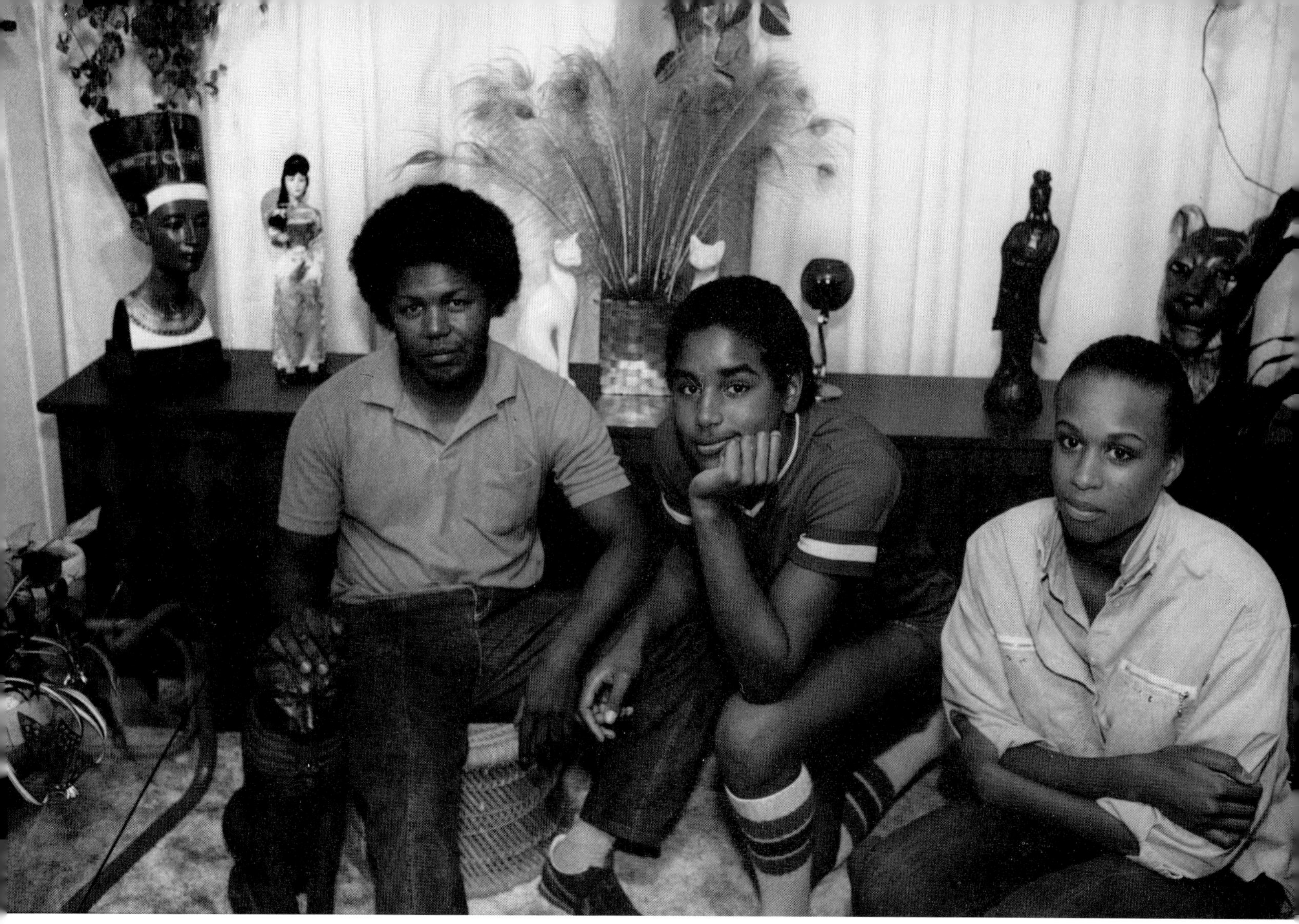

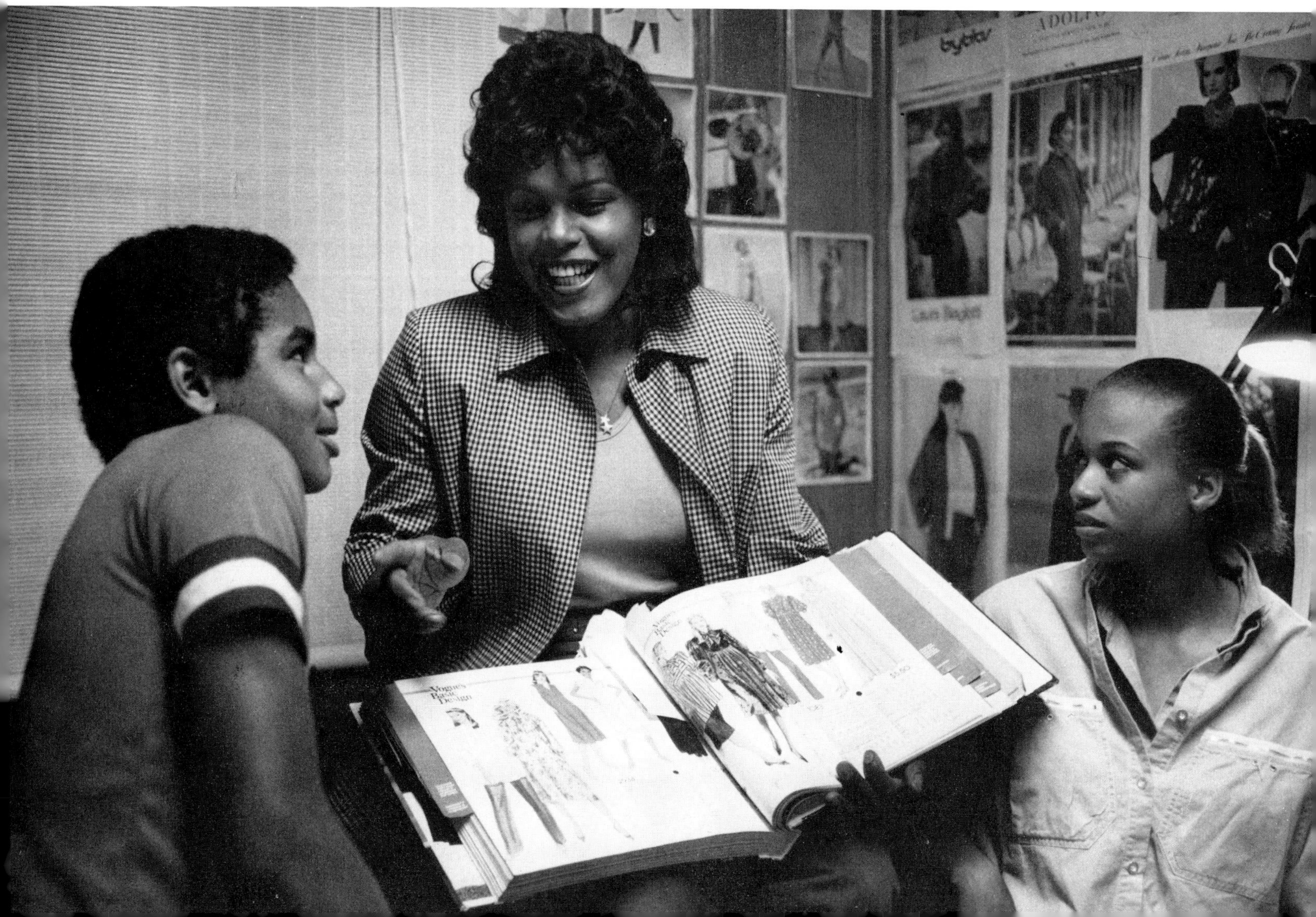
byblos

Joe, Joe Jr., and stepdaughter Jackie

to crossdress again. I left school to teach broadcasting, and there I met this attractive black woman. Oh, she just turned me on! She was Buddhist, like me. We'd been engaged a year before I told her about my crossdressing.

I was twenty when we started living together, and I became stepfather to her three girls. I wasn't prepared for all this, and when our son was born it ruined my bank account. I got an agent, and began working in movies and commercials. I was crossdressing secretly—I had a darkroom in the basement, where I kept all my clothes. I'd crossdress, and suddenly I'd have a tremendous amount of energy. My wife went into my darkroom one day and found all my stuff. I'd kept the magazines I had gotten from porn shops, because they were the closest thing I had to finding out who I was or seeing somebody who did what I did. To prove my manhood to her, to prove that I wasn't going to do this anymore, I *burned* it all in the fireplace. I purged three times. Hundreds of dollars' worth of magazines and clothes. Eventually we divorced.

My wife wanted me to be the one to dish out the punishment, and I couldn't. So the kids and I would pretend. I would hit myself, and they would just scream. The only one I ever really hit was the boy, 'cause boys are supposed to be able to take that shit. Tough, right? Bunch of bullshit! I've been brainwashed.

Aside from dressing for masturbation, I dress now only when I'm really pushed in a corner. Diahanna doesn't have any responsibilities. She doesn't have children. She doesn't have parents. She doesn't have *anything* to be concerned about. Diahanna smokes, and Joe doesn't. Diahanna can handle more liquor than Joe. It's like zipping off one jumpsuit and putting on a different one. Diahanna's a *character*, she's not a woman. She's the one who can say words like "caress." She can say loving things to people and not have to hide. She can touch someone lovingly or softly without gripping them. I created her within the realm of whatever my limitations might be.

I now give myself permission to seek others who might be doing the same thing. I'm doing more talking and making appearances, and I'm dressing now only for those occasions. It's like an extension of the theater. The play I never got to do. Presenting myself publicly is probably the strongest and riskiest thing I've ever done in my life.

JOE JR. (DIAHANNA'S SON)

I found out about my father's crossdressing seven years ago. He told me, I watched him dress for a while, and then he came out of his room as Diahanna. I thought it was someone else. He said, "Joe, it's me!" I backed up so far I hit the couch and fell down. Another time I saw him dressed, and started laughing. I thought of myself wearing a miniskirt! Some of the kids at school have seen my father on television, and one kid said, "Your father's a fag." I said, "He's not a fag!" I pushed him and he went tumbling down some stairs.

There's someone at school who dresses, and he thought he was going crazy. My friend Lamont knows about my father, and told the kid to talk to me. I said something like, "If it's a part of you that you want to express, express it. It's not a problem. Just try to make a go of it."

Joe Jr., Joe as Diahanna, and Jackie

JAN (DIAHANNA'S GIRLFRIEND)

I like being able to introduce Joe as "This is my boyfriend. He's one of the most beautiful women I've ever seen!" To me, the appeal is that you can appear as a woman, with painted toenails, nylons, and makeup, and not be a helpless pushover. I love the stereotypes it blows away. I'm inspired by those people who insist on doing what they have to do, at great potential cost to themselves.

When I go to a party at ETVC [a transvestite-transsexual club in San Francisco], I wonder, What are they like in their daily male work life? It brings out how society chokes people. *You* go to this trap called male, *you* go to this trap called female. Out of these traps, we have all the options.

Diahanna: "Diahanna's a character, she's not a woman. I created her within the realm of whatever my limitations might be."

VITO-LINDA

I was born to a middle-class super-Italian family, the only boy growing up with ten girls, some sisters, some cousins. I have pictures of myself, three years old, wearing a dress. I always had the feeling of being a woman. When they separated me from the girls at around age seven, I was very distraught. This confusion led me to use heroin when I was about twelve. I was an addict for years. Robbing, fighting, carrying weapons, getting arrested. During all this, I was crossdressing. I was also performing as a jazz and rock-and-roll musician, solo and in bands. I've been playing the piano since I was ten; my aunt was a piano teacher.

I ended up in Daytop [a drug rehabilitation facility], got my act straightened out, came back out, still had the gender problem, and was still denying it. The more I denied it, the worse I swung toward a grotesque manifestation of what I thought a man was. I acted out a strange conglomeration of James Cagney movies. I became the director of Samaritan House [another drug rehabilitation program], but then got back into the drugs again. I met Abby through drugs; she was involved, too. Here she thought she'd hooked up with Al Capone's reincarnation, but within a week of living with me, I put on a dress and a wig!

My plan was to make a whole lot of money and have a sex-change operation. I ended up getting very strung out, wound up in the hospital for a kidney operation, lost a lot of money, and was out on the street. Abby and I were drinking in the street, strung out on heroin, sleeping on people's floors. I took hormones and freaked out, gained a hundred pounds and grew a beard. Finally, sometime in our mid-thirties, we kinda settled in. We stopped drinking and smoking and doing drugs. I'm going through electrolysis, I'm on hormones, and we've moved to a really tolerant community where I can be whoever I want to be. I play the piano at a restaurant. I'm not as nervous and confused as I used to be. I feel a lot better.

ABBY (VITO-LINDA'S MATE)

My mother came from a strict New England family and my father was a southern partier, an alcoholic woman-chaser. They got divorced when I was ten. I had very little contact with my father after that, and my mother taught me that he was an evil person. During my

Vito-Linda and mate, Abby: "Vito and Linda are the same person inside—lipstick and the kind of shoes are the only difference."

Madeline Victoria–Retired Police Officer

Paula and daughter Lisa

Valerie—Scientist with many patents

Dorothy–Former Captain, British Royal Navy

Cynthia and wife, Nina

Vanessa–Computer Operator, Amateur Guitarist

Candace–Audio Technician

Felicity–Aviator, at 79, and at 5

Kay–Ex-Green Beret

Kary and daughter Dana

Elaine–Inventor, Researcher

Joe—Artist and Mechanic

Joe as Diahanna

Terisa—Financial Analyst and Science Fiction Writer.

Andy becoming Andi

Ken becoming Kathy

Ken becoming Kathy

Gwen—Musician, with brother Hugh and sister-in-law, Pam

twenties, I went through a very strong rebellion against my mother. I felt she had given me a warped attitude about men. For about ten years, I became my father's child—if my father is evil and untrustworthy, then I must be, too. So I was wild, crazy, experimenting with drugs and the hippie lifestyle, living in Europe. When I met Vito-Linda, sixteen years ago, he said, "There's something very important I have to tell you about myself—I'm really a woman!" I said, "Oh great!," because I really didn't want to hook up with somebody who was an ordinary man. I'd been married, and had had a stormy relationship with somebody who had other girlfriends, like my father. I felt I couldn't have committed myself to a real man. I was relieved and happy even though I wasn't quite sure what he meant. When I saw him in the wig and dress, that comforted me a lot, it gave me a feeling of hope for the future of the relationship.

I made a commitment in the beginning of the relationship to help Vito become Linda. I thought it would take seven years. At the end of seven years, she was no closer to coming out than when we met. It's been a harder struggle than I thought it would be for Linda to materialize. Vito and Linda are the same person inside—lipstick and the kind of shoes are the only difference. Vito-Linda is the person I love. I am not defined by the sex of the person I am with. Sexual fascination wears off; there has to be something deeper. Who a person is, what they believe. Vito-Linda is my soul mate.

RACHEL

I feel that my true self is Rachel. I grew up introverted. As Rachel, I am much more outgoing, to the point of being an exhibitionist. I started to come out when I began working weekends as a waitress in a bar owned by a transsexual. Soon I was drawn into performing in shows, and the extrovert was born.

My emerging personality, lifestyle, and dressing style come from my attraction to the S&M [sadism and masochism] scene. Leather clothing, heavy-metal music. I love the feeling of tight-fitting stretch clothes. The tightness is associated with bondage and submission in S&M. I enjoy the attention I get, and I dress to make a strong impression, to shock.

S&M and B&D [bondage and discipline] in my life involve the mental and emotional attraction and bond to a dominant person, and physical restraint [cuffs, chains, leather implements]. Over the years I've had several dominant submissive relationships. My first was with a female impersonator whom I served as her slave-maid. My most intense relationship with a dominant has been with a "she-male" who has a dungeon in her home. I've had numerous sessions there involving the use of restraint and punishment devices. These experiences have been extremely satisfying, both emotionally and physically, and have increased my desire to live this way full-time. In fact, she asked me to be her full-time slave, but I couldn't bring myself to leave my job in retail, and although I am divorced after twelve years of marriage, I didn't want to lose contact with my ex-wife and child.

My most recent contact is with a female who enjoys acting as a dominant. I feel that we will work well together as a dominant-submissive couple. I'm drawn toward long-term relationships in which I am bound to the other person mentally as a submissive.

Rachel and her girlfriend, Marsha. Rachel: "My dressing style comes from my attraction to the S&M scene. I enjoy the attention I get, and I dress to make a strong impression, to shock."

DEE

My mother started dressing me as a girl when I was about five years old. Her excuse was that we lived in Jersey City, in a rough neighborhood, and she didn't want me going out. I'd come home from school, and she'd have clothes laid out for me. If I objected, she'd put dark red lipstick or bright nail polish on me—things I couldn't take off easily. Other times, she'd sit me down and teach me to put on makeup. Every Halloween, she dressed me up and showed me off to her friends. She made me try on dresses in stores, claiming they were for my cousin. The ladies in the stores thought it was the cutest thing! My father left when I was three and I hardly ever saw him, so he never knew what was going on at home.

When I was about ten, my older sister got involved in dressing me, too. Her girlfriends came over, and they'd dress me and take me out. I had very few boy friends; my mother discouraged it. Before she got her beautician's license, my mother used me to practice hair setting, manicures, makeup. By then, I stopped pretending to resent it. I started to like dressing as a girl, although I always wanted people to know I was a boy. I played baseball as a kid, and did other normal boy things, but if a girl walked by who was really dressed nice, my mind would wander off and I'd run home and dress up.

When I was a teenager, I bought my own clothes and I'd go out alone at night. One day, I saw this boy with makeup walk by. I never knew there was anyone else like me. We became friends, and then lovers. I assumed I was gay, and that this is what I was supposed to do. He was in with a group of boys who dressed up, and they wore makeup and blouses but no padding. They didn't want to be taken for girls. They were mostly Cuban and spoke hardly any English. I was the only Anglo, and I fit in with this group for a few years. In this club were women who liked these boys, and they got them going in a step-by-step process toward total feminization. It was like initiation rights into a sorority. They started out with light makeup and clear nail polish and progressed to complete makeup, hairdo, tweezed eyebrows.

When I graduated from high school, I started working at my mother's beauty salon. I wore my hair and nails very long, had tweezed eyebrows, and acted very effeminate. She told me I had to change, that the customers didn't like it. I went to a school to become an electrician to make money. I wanted a change. I married a woman I met in high school and now we've got four children, two sons and two daughters. It never entered my mind to dress my sons as daughters, even though my sister does it to her own son. My nephew is fourteen and does it to himself now.

My wife knows very little about my crossdressing. We both wear teddies to bed at night. I made her think it was her idea—if I wore nail polish on my toes and had shaved legs, that would keep me from fooling around! When we were first married, my wife went to work, and sometimes I'd take the day off and go to Bamberger's. Or at night I'd go to New York to the Gilded Grape or G.G. Barnum's to be with my friends. I always thought if you dressed, you had to be outrageous; you couldn't just do it normally. Now I hardly do it anymore. I work nights, she's home with the kids days. I'm thirty-seven, and I can't let everyone know that I'm a boy in a dress, like I did when I was seventeen.

All my life I've felt different from other people. It has taken me many years to understand what happened to me. I'm glad it did. I've had a lot of fun. It's like being two people. I learned to live two lives.

Dee—a Factory Worker. "I played baseball as a kid, but if a girl walked by who was really dressed nice, my mind would wander off and I'd run home and dress up."

GWEN

One of my earliest memories occurred when I was six. My brother Hugh was an actor with the Living Theater in New York, and he came home to visit. He talked about his life there and at one point said, "The entire cast of the theater was invited to a party recently, and Christine Jorgensen was there." Well, my mother knew she'd heard the name before but couldn't quite place it, so my brother said, "You know, that guy who changed his sex!" It clicked! I remember thinking, almost as though it were a Polaroid in my mind, That's me! I should be a girl.

I remember one time, I took red food coloring and rubbed it into my lips. If I dyed my lips permanently red, they'd have to let me be a girl. Every night I'd go to bed and pray that when I woke up I'd be transformed. I couldn't understand why my prayers went unanswered.

By the time I was thirteen I'd stolen a copy of the book *The Transsexual Phenomenon*. I was too embarrassed to be caught buying it. As a result of reading it, I knew that puberty was upon me. In a last-ditch effort to have my feelings taken seriously before the "Testosterone Monster" reared its ugly head, I skipped school one day and dressed in a black skirt and blouse of my mother's. I also wore a black pillbox hat and gloves. I must have looked like I was attending a funeral. Maybe I thought I was! I took a bus across town to one of the hospitals, located the psychiatric ward, walked up to the receptionist, and said, "Hi, I'm a transsexual. I want to talk to somebody." I spoke to a doctor, and he had my mother pick me up. She took me home, and told me that she now believed I was serious about wanting to be a girl, and that she'd be willing to share her post-menopause hormone pills with me! From reading that book, I had a pretty good idea of a proper dosage, so for quite a while, we shared her estrogen.

One of my most horrid memories occurred shortly after the hospital adventure. One night, as I was sitting home dressed in female clothes, my mother came in drunk, with two or three of her drinking buddies. She apparently still felt this type of embarrassment might shock me into more appropriate behavior. She said something like, "This is my son. He likes to wear girl's clothes!" I was mortified. I felt my most sacred trust had been ripped open and probed.

Gwen and her mother, Shirley: "A psychiatrist suggested to me that I give Gwen up for adoption. There's no way I'd give my baby up! I love her like you wouldn't believe."

On April 25, 1979, I took the step that I'd been leading up to my entire life. I returned from performing as a musician in Europe with the U.S.O., and the very next day, Gwen was, in essence, born. On October 22, 1979, I legally became a female. In fact, I was one of the first individuals able to have such measures taken without having had sexual reassignment surgery. My transition from male to female was fairly easy. Many of my friends have quizzed me about how to pass as female, and I never know what to tell them. If there was a formula, and I knew it, I'd be rich! I think it was easy for me because I spent the first twenty-five years of my life studying for the part.

Recently, I decided to see if I could still pass as a man, so I went out with Mariette and allowed her to shoot my little experiment. I couldn't seem to get the male walk right, and I felt like everybody was staring at me. Just as my confidence began to return, she had an encounter with some punk rockers who objected to her taking their photo. Well, I was beginning to feel pretty butch by this time, and in my most assertive tone said, "No way is

Gwen and her mate, Colleen. Gwen: "I was engaged to a man for a while, then I realized that I wasn't attracted to men at all"
Colleen: "I see Gwen and I relate to her as my lover, my girlfriend, as a woman."

Gwen crossdressed as Patrick: "I don't know if I can say what it is to be a woman. One of the things it is, is a struggle."

she going to pay you, or give you her film!" I took her arm, and as we turned to walk away I heard one of the guys say to the other, "Dykes!"

The most significant event in my life was when Colleen entered the picture. She's the only person in the world for whom I'd give up living as a woman, but I don't anticipate that happening. To this day, I can evoke her laughter just by relating some of my "macho" past. She can't believe I ever passed as a man! If she hadn't accepted me as I am, I would still be convinced that my anatomical "irregularity" was keeping me from finding some-

Gwen—Musician: "I no longer need to wear androgynously styled clothing, or sensible shoes as part of my feminist persona."

one. Her love made the puzzle of my life complete. Colleen was the missing piece.

I define myself as a lesbian, and many people don't understand that, including some lesbians. They feel that transsexual or transgendered people defining themselves as lesbian is perhaps the most blatant example of men usurping their space. I'm a lesbian because I believe it's the best way I can manifest change in society's attitudes about not only women's liberation, but men's as well. As a feminist, I've found a balance between what I believe politically and how I choose to present myself. I struggle every day to avoid being socialized into perpetuating the stereotyped roles forced on women. I'm appalled and insulted when I see the way many crossdressers and other gender-conflicted people present themselves. The concept of woman as "slut" or "hooker" offends me.

My life has been so goofy, but I wouldn't trade with anybody. I think that when it's over I'll be able to say, "It couldn't have been better!"

COLLEEN (GWEN'S MATE)

I felt a little more special when she trusted me enough to tell me such a personal part of her past. Our relationship as lovers didn't begin until much later. Gwen was still testing out some waters with dating men. We double-dated!

I see Gwen, and I relate to her as my lover, my girlfriend, a woman. When we first became lovers, Gwen was planning to have reassignment surgery. She's since decided it isn't necessary, and basically, it doesn't matter to me. I love her personality, and how she takes care of me, and how she is with other people. She's got a goodness in her heart. Our life, and our love life, is like a special little fantasy world that we've made for ourselves. It's just tailor-made for us.

Gwen

We've talked about having a child. I'm not thrilled with the concept of being pregnant, but I can't go down to Kmart and pick one out! The technicalities of our having a child are awesome. We're still talking about it.

I've got the best of both worlds. She's the best thing that ever happened in my life.

SHIRLEY (GWEN'S MOTHER)

I wanted a little girl, and before her birth I used to rub my tummy and talk to her. When she was born and the doctor held him up he said, "Another boy!" I said, "Put him back. I've already got a boy! I want a little girl!"

One night I woke up about four o'clock in the morning and she wasn't home. I knew she was dressing as a girl. From then on, to keep her from going out at night, I'd sit in her doorway with my feet across the beam so she'd have to step over me.

As a man, she was built like an Adonis. I was hoping Patrick would grow up, get married and give me some grandchildren. Instead, she just wanted to be a lady. One day, I got home from work and she had written me a letter that literally tore my soul apart, about mother love, and how she needed someone that she could talk to. After that, I didn't fight her anymore. I helped her in any way I could. She began taking hormones when she was thirteen. I accepted her as my daughter.

My heart is broken, though, because nobody remembers my little boy, Patrick. Only I remember Patrick. And I miss him, 'cause I loved him. I still do. But he's gone.

Gwen

There's not any part of him left. That mischievous, mean, gettin'-into-trouble kid is gone. When I look at pictures of Patrick, it makes me cry for him. I'm always wondering, What if . . . ?

HUGH (GWEN'S BROTHER)

I was thirteen when Gwen was born, and the family was really beginning to come apart. Our father had always been an alcoholic, and after Gwen was born our mother started to drink a lot, too.

    I was concerned and confused about Gwen's behavior. I didn't know what to think of the fact that my brother was walking around the neighborhood in women's clothes. Now, I think it's great! I think Gwen is, in a way, representative of the godhead. She represents the unification of opposites. Actually, it's better than that. It seems to me that one of the biggest problems we have in our society is that everybody's polarized, and suffering mightily. What they need is to become whole, complete human beings. Gwen has resolved that in her own unique way. I think that the Higher Power is not at all polarized on the right or the left, but is rather all-encompassing. And on a sexual level, so is Gwen. I think that she's a very valuable, national treasure.

NAOMI

SWJM, 52, J.D./Atty.; TV, Fem, Fat and Fun; Into: Photography, Antique Silver, Foreign Travel and Women's Clothes. There's a little bit of theater in Naomi.

For twenty years I suppressed my desires to crossdress, living only for the Halloween Ball each year. At one of the balls, I met a group of crossdressers. They seemed like decent, respectable people with families and careers. They invited me to a party where I met Ariadne Kane, the founder of Fantasia Fair, who just happened to be visiting in town. At this point, I owned no female clothes, but I had the best camera equipment. She invited me to come to Fantasia Fair to be the official photographer. I asked Ariadne, "If I come, do I have to dress?" She responded, "No, but maybe you would like to."

    I bought enough clothes for the nine days, and off I went. My idea was that by the end of the Fair I would either like it or hate it. When I went home that year my feet were so swollen I could hardly put on my men's shoes; my earlobes hurt; and thanks to the wig, I felt like I had been wearing a hat for a week. But I knew this was something that I couldn't resist. I was hooked! Since then, I've become very active in the crossdressing community. In addition to my legal practice, I'm president of a midwestern chapter of the crossdressing sorority, Tri-Ess (Society for the Second Self).

    In 1980, while at a local wig shop, I met a very special lady. She, of course, knew about my crossdressing but didn't really understand why I did such a thing. For that matter, neither do I. She saw something else in me that she liked. She became my best friend and lover.

Naomi, a lawyer, and a Jewish princess

BARBARA

In first grade, a girl in our class was warming her fingers under her bangs while reading in a cold classroom. The following was my thought sequence:
"If I had long hair, I could keep my fingers warm too!"
"If I had long hair and wore a dress, I would be a girl!"
"If I were a girl, Hank couldn't tease me into wanting to kill him, because in our family girls are not teased or beaten up!"

From September 1940 to September 1941 I was an officer on the USS *Brooklyn*. We cruised the North Atlantic, and our destroyers attacked and sank two German submarines. This action earned all of us an "A" to be worn on the American Defense Ribbon denoting "Action in the Atlantic—Prior to Pearl Harbor." I ended up in Washington, D.C., eventually rising to Officer in Charge of Research and Development at the Naval Code and Signal Lab. I learned at the lab that I was an inventor, which I hadn't known before. My most important invention, which saved countless lives and shortened the European war, was a device based on the cipher machine recovered from a German submarine.

Years after the war and five children later, my wife discovered my secret. She was counseled by an ignorant psychiatrist that my desire would become stronger and stronger until I would be "walking the streets of our neighborhood, dressed as a woman."

The family spent two months each year at our summer home in Michigan, and that is when I was able to dress. When my wife discovered I hadn't quit my hobby, she broke into my locked closet, with a locksmith's help, and got rid of everything! My clothing, wigs, and photographs dating back to 1937. "You have killed half of me!" [I said.]

I found a better hiding place and accumulated another wardrobe. I took a feminine name, Barbara. It was the name of my first serious girlfriend, and my wife had always been jealous of her!

My first wife died in November of 1977, and over a year later I was still lonely even with the help of my alter ego, Barbara. I met my present wife, a romance flourished, and we were married in 1979. My earlier mistake was not repeated, and my wife not only knew about Barbara, she saw her a good deal before we were even engaged. She encouraged me to attend Tri-Ess. Since then, it has been my pleasurable, self-imposed task to ease the entry of other "first-timers" into *their* new world.

My brother Hank died this summer. His childhood domination over me and my screams of anger and frustration are hidden within me. However, if his teasing and bullying were in any way responsible for my becoming part-time Barbara, I am ever grateful to him. It has given me the most exquisitely wonderful pleasure I think can be known, except for the intimate pleasure between my wife and me.

Barbara bares her natural bosom

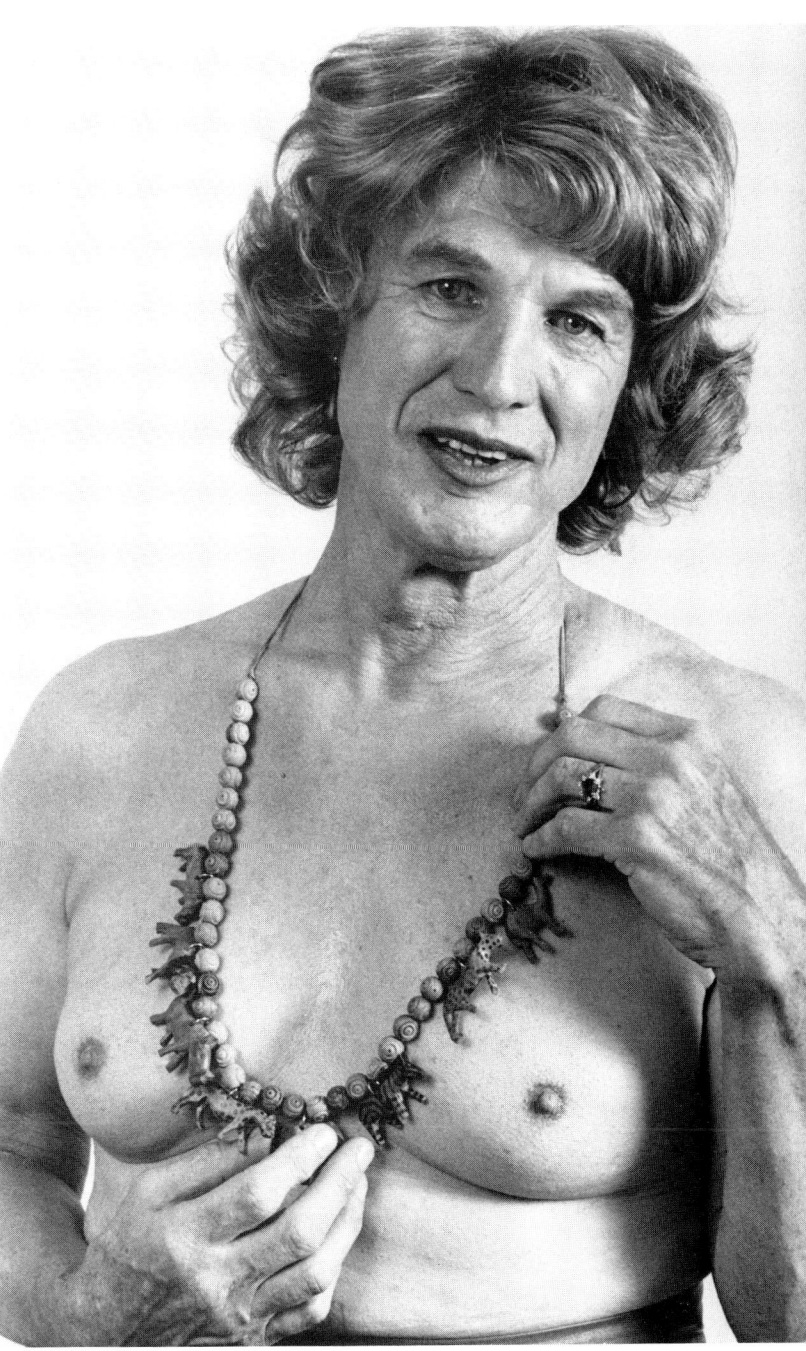

"Daddy" Chrysis and Nicole. Chrysis: "I saw that women were treated better, more soft and gentle. They got the prettier things."

CHRYSIS

When I was a child, I felt hurt that I couldn't be a girl. I just wanted to escape from my dad's beatings. I noticed many times that my sister rarely got spanked. She got talked to, and sent to her room. I'd be sent to my room and told to pull down my pants and wait. Sometimes the whole night would go by, and I'd still be waiting with my pants down until Mom would come in and say, "You go ahead and go to bed, your dad has passed out." My brothers and I would just lie in terror hoping that he wouldn't remember what he wanted to beat us for. And when he did beat me, he became furious that I wouldn't cry. I'd just lie there and take the beating, and when it was over I'd just glare at him and pray that someday he'd keel over and die.

My mom was confined to a wheelchair while I was growing up. I'd always help her get dressed for her nights out. I wanted her to look really beautiful and proud of herself even though she was in a wheelchair. I wanted her to know that she was still a woman, no matter what! I'd help her on and off the bedpan. I ran the water, and put her in the tub, and scrubbed her back for her. I can remember doing all this as far back as when I was four years old. I pulled her panty girdle up and hooked her corset. I tried to cinch it up as tight as I could, with all the snaps and zippers. Then I'd get her hose hooked up and make sure the seams were straight, and get her shoes on. She had a lot of dresses that were low-cut, with spaghetti straps, and maybe that's why I like to wear those same kinds of dresses. I always wanted to be like Mom. I liked this ritual of getting Mom ready; helping her get dressed for the evening was the happiest time of my childhood.

I remember being bathed by my aunts at my grandmother's house, and afterward being dressed as a girl by them. I started getting female clothes by going through backyards and alleyways, taking them off the clotheslines, not even knowing if they'd fit or not.

I started shoplifting when I was in the seventh grade. During high school I was doing a lot of breaking into stores, mainly for cigarettes and things like that. All this was to impress my friends and to show them that I was a "guy." After high school I started breaking into homes. I spent some time in the California Youth Authority.

Nicole, Chrysis, and Barbara at home in Happy Acres trailer park. Beyond the fences surrounding the park, cowboys ride over the hills getting ready for the rodeo.

I've never been tough. I've tried to act tough. I've always tried to talk my way out of situations, and if I can't, I'll resort to physical violence. I have a friend named Eddie, and he knows me as Chrysis, and has accepted me as Chrysis, but he *knows* that he doesn't want to mess with me, 'cause I'll just come out of my "girl bag" and put on my "man bag" and just whip all over him.

After I left the service, I went back to breaking into homes again. I was arrested twice. The first time, I was caught in a house with a couple of bags filled with all the female clothing I could load into them. Intimate apparel, swimwear, shorts, and tops. After three years, I was still doing the same thing. Later, I committed another burglary while on probation and was sentenced to prison for five years to life, and was paroled after serving five years. I knew that it was a crime to break into someone's home, but I needed the clothing. I didn't have any idea that I could go to a department store and purchase the clothing for myself. And I really didn't have the finances to do it.

I met Barbara when she was fifteen, but she was a lot older in her mind, how she thought about things. I was attracted to her openness and her caring. I've always needed somebody to care for me and to be with me. I saw a lot of hurt in her eyes. She just wanted somebody to love her and to treat her like a person, and to teach her more than she knew. I wanted to buy her things, clothes, shoes, whatever I could. Show her how to put on makeup, give her a little more out of life.

Barbara and I have talked about how to deal with my crossdressing as our daughter, Nicole, gets older, and we've decided to talk to her and let her understand how we feel. And then she has the right to either approve or disapprove of it. And if my dressing in any way hurts her, or if it interferes with us having friends, then I would cease my dressing in public. I would probably continue secretly.

BARBARA (CHRYSIS'S WIFE)

I really prefer Chrysis as a woman. I feel strongly that she should dress as a female. I don't want him to ever change. I want us to always be as sisters and lovers. I don't see him as male when he's dressed, or when he's not dressed. Even though he has the part that is male, he's not like a man.

My father left me and my sister and two older brothers when I was about a year old. Mom never did explain why Dad left. But I have a feeling that it was because of her drinking. My stepfather drank, too. He pushed me toward a friend of his . . . he raped me. I just feel like killing my stepfather sometimes.

Those memories are always there. That's why we feel so much pain and don't ever want Nicole to have something like that happen. We want her to grow up and have a mother or dad, or mother and auntie, to love.

FELICITY

I was born in 1905. My mother was hoping for a girl, but I arrived with the opposite plumbing. I had a younger sister and a still younger brother, and we all got along even though we had entirely different interests.

In accordance with the custom of the day, I had my hair in a short bob until age five and a half. Before having it cut, in June of 1911, my mother dressed me in the clothes of a girl who lived across the street, complete with hair ribbon, and had my dad take photos of me, much to my embarrassment. From then on, I was proud of my short hair.

About that time I saw an airplane for the first time, and from that day on I was determined to become an aviator. The result was a long and successful aviation career that continues even now, seven decades later.

At age twelve, I came across those photos my father took. They revived my memory of the event and irresistibly rekindled my interest in crossdressing.

At age twenty-six I confided in my fiancée about my crossdressing and disclosed myself to her while dressed. To my surprise, she accepted and told me she'd been an ardent fan of the famous female impersonator Julian Eltinge. A little later I found the word "transvestite" defined. I researched the subject in the library and discovered that I was not alone in the "underground."

We were married for thirty years and had three children and some grandchildren before she died. Although I was six foot two, we could wear each other's clothes, since she was about five foot seven and size eighteen.

After two years of bachelorhood, I remarried, and Eleanor and I have been together almost eighteen years now. I disclosed my crossdressing to her before marriage, and being an exceptionally bright person, she accepted it and cooperated fully.

We have a normal sex life, even though we're senior citizens. The clothes have no erotic effect on me, though I do know of crossdressers who admit to it. Crossdressing gets me out of the drab, monotonous masculine uniform and into the infinite variety that is the exclusive territory of women. I love to trespass in their world. Poaching in a feminine paradise. Men's departments are dens of depression; women's departments are palaces and flower gardens.

When I discovered those childhood photos, they brought back the memory of that light and cool fluttering dress, and the sensation of being pretty myself. Those sensations have never left me. Nor do I wish them to. Crossdressing is a pastime that has afforded me thousands of hours of contentment, happiness, pleasure, and relaxation. I selected the name Felicity Chandelle because "felicity" means a state of happiness and well-being, and "chandelle" means a candle for the enlightened. No pastime holds a candle to being Felicity!

Felicity—Aviator and Great-grandfather at 79, and at 5.
"When I discovered this childhood photo, it brought back the memory of that light and cool fluttering dress, and the sensation of being pretty myself."

LYNDA

I remember being very close to my mother when I was little. My father was never around. He worked long hours. He was in the live poultry business. I started crossdressing in puberty, but it didn't go away as I thought it would once I started having regular sex—it just goes through cycles where it's stronger and weaker. During the four years I was in the service after high school it disappeared completely. I came back home to Brooklyn. I was sure it would go away once I got married. I was a wild kid. Very active. I had a lot of dates, did a lot of drinking, a lot of running around.

I waited ten years after we were married before telling Rebecca. What I did, accidentally on purpose—subconsciously—is I left a bra in a drawer. Rebecca found it and thought I was having an affair. When I told her, she went out and bought all these porno magazines that had pictures of lesbians, to try to get used to the idea of having sex with me as a woman. The only clue she had had was a number of years before that when we had gone to the Jewel Box Review, which was a really good female impersonator show—my mother was actually selling tickets from the synagogue for it—and when we came home, as she was getting undressed, I asked her if she would let me put her girdle on. She thought I was kidding. When she saw I wasn't, she was really upset. That kept me from saying anything to her for a long time.

For the next ten or fifteen years, I kept the crossdressing very low-key. Some panties under male clothes, but never fully dressed. It was very important to me that Rebecca accept it, and that was all she could take. When I got to be fifty, and my friends began to pass away, I said to myself it would just be a terrible thing if I were to live my whole life and die and not have done the one thing I most terribly wanted to do all my life—to dress fully. It just wouldn't be fair.

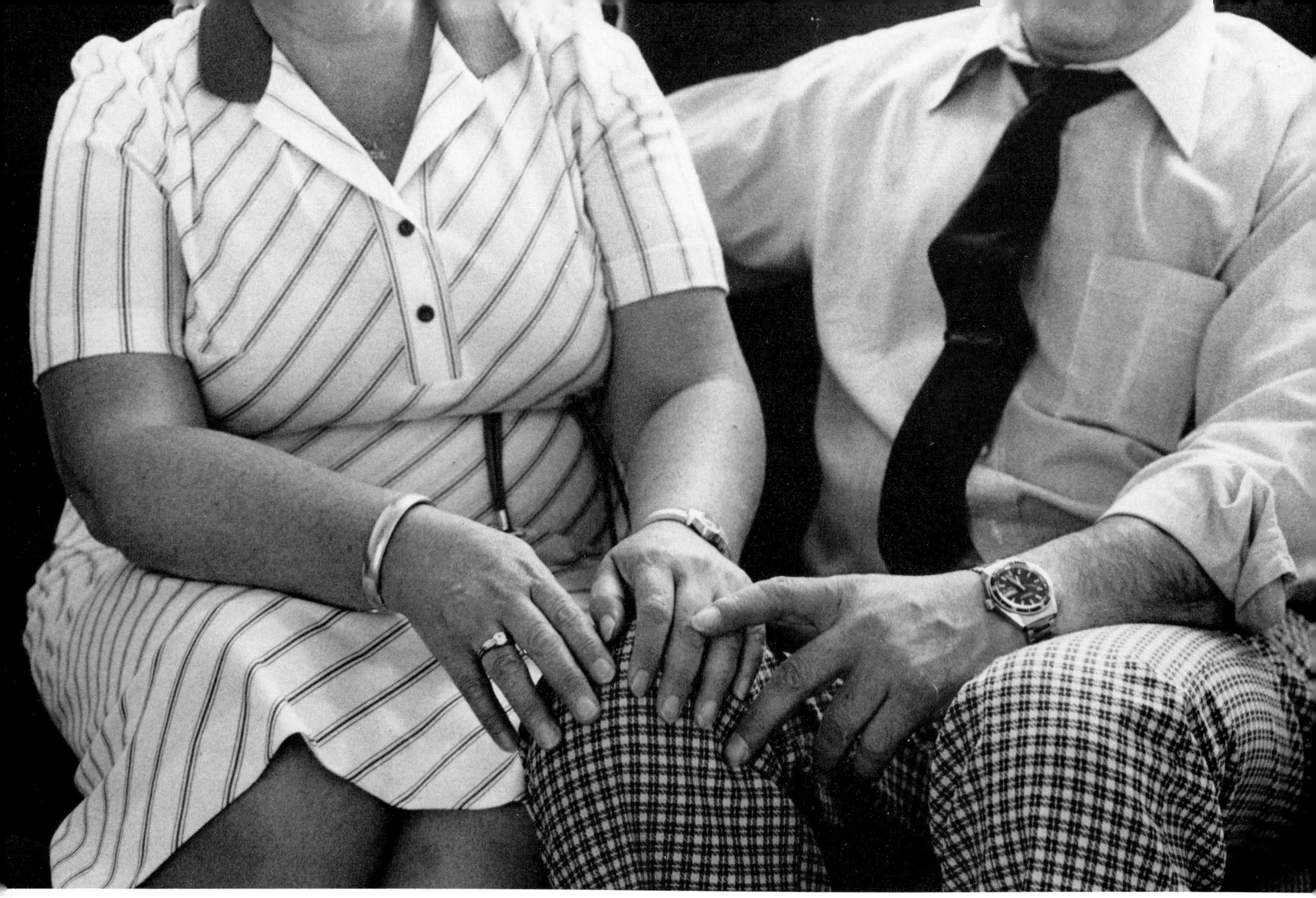

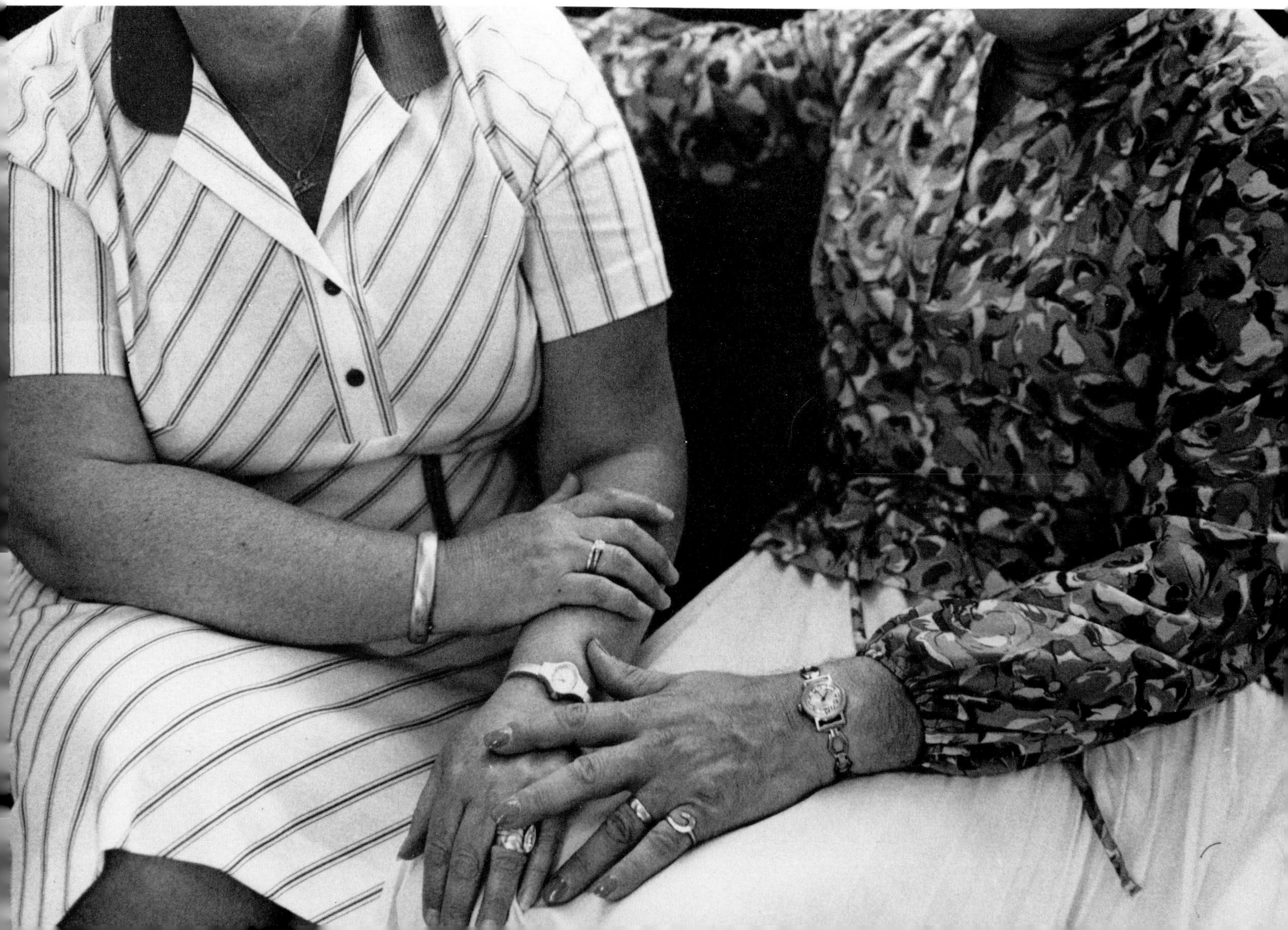

Rebecca and Ben

At that point I started to search around. I'd never met any other crossdressers. I found a therapist, Garrett Oppenheim, who ran a group for people in all stages of transsexualism and transvestism. I wanted information, not on the physical part of dressing, but on reasons for it. Why am I this way? Where will it go? What does it mean? I knew I wanted to dress and pass as a woman. It took two years, going to meetings twice a month, before Rebecca got to the point where she would come too. That took us to Fantasia Fair, where we learned a lot, and Rebecca was part of the partner support group. My fears were finally put to rest when Virginia Prince told me this was something I could control, that it would go as far as I wanted it to go. My crossdressing won't jeopardize what I hold important in my life. Besides my family and my job, I'm active in our local synagogue, the town planning board, and the Rotary Club. Rebecca works with me and she runs the temple bingo game and Helpline, taking calls from people in need of support for all kinds of things, even sometimes a crossdresser or crossdresser's wife!

Lynda with grandson Wayne. "When my grandson saw Lynda for the first time, he said, 'Hi, Pop-Pop!' I guess there's no fooling kids."

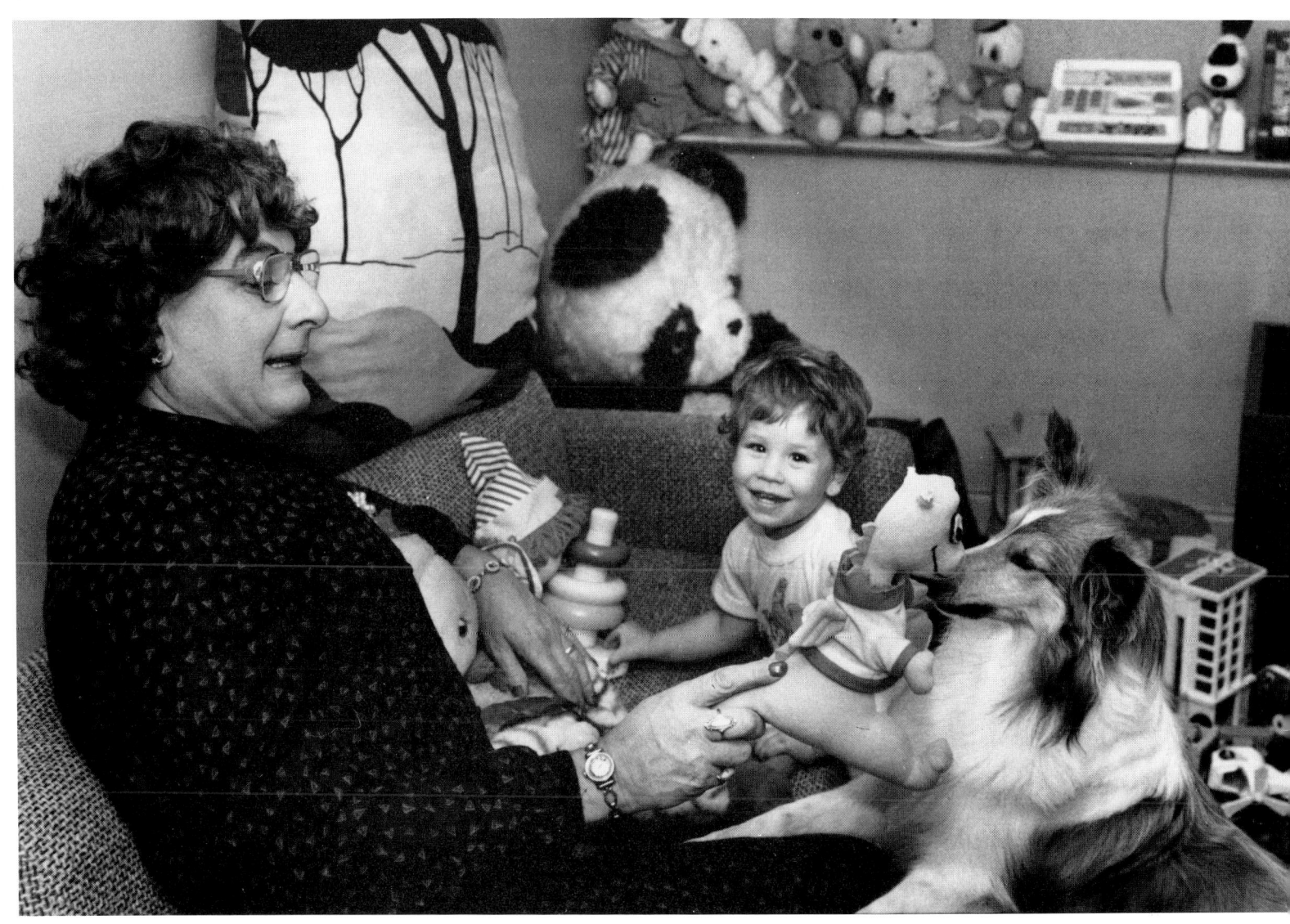

Rebecca and her husband, Ben, as Lynda

Recently we told our three children. They all think Rebecca's fantastic for putting up with it. I guess the kids feel that if Rebecca doesn't have a problem with it, they don't have the right to have a problem either. When she told our son, Stan, he said, "Things are going so great for me in my life that I'm kind of pleased. I need a little twist!" When his son Wayne, my grandson, saw Lynda for the first time, he said, "Hi, Pop-Pop!" I guess there's no fooling kids.

Wayne with "Pop-Pop" Lynda

MALINDA

When I was growing up, often I would stare deeply into the mirror and ask, "Why?" Thirty years later I look into the mirror and ask the same question.

It wasn't until high school that I found the word "transvestite" in a book on abnormal sexuality, and the guilt was incredible! You'll never know the inner pain of a fifteen-year-old boy in a small, football-oriented midwestern town, who must try to compete in a super-masculine atmosphere, knowing all the time that he is weak, unworthy, and separate from others. Those who knew me well observed that even as a child I had a space within me clearly marked private.

After high school, instead of attending college I opted to travel. History, art, and literature were strong interests of mine, so I prowled the museums of Europe. At nineteen I became very religious. I attended a Lutheran school and then became a Bahai, a member of Universalist religion that preaches against prejudice. I even went to Africa, to the fringe of the Kalahari Desert as a missionary to help spread these Universalist teachings. I became involved with a woman to whom I confided about my crossdressing. This backfired when I found out she ran around telling all my friends. I couldn't handle it, and I later attempted suicide with an overdose of sleeping tablets. I went home, put TVism out of my mind, grew a beard, and tried to live a quiet life.

I met someone via a TV correspondence magazine who changed my life. We met at a hotel, where she made me up. When I looked in the mirror and saw myself for the first time with a flawless makeup job, attractive clothing, and wig, my heart literally stopped! At last I knew my cherished desire had become reality. It was obvious I made a much-better-looking woman than a man. This episode put me on a narcissistic binge lasting more than a decade. Sharon also took me to Chicago for my first, but not last, tour of drag bars.

I started going out in public, and came to the conclusion that it was time for me to follow my star wherever it led. My speed in coming out caused me a few problems. I drank too much on occasion, and I got involved with prostitution in Chicago, where I worked as a B-girl in a drag bar. Now I only crossdress for public appearances. It's too boring to do it at home. It's like playing a musical instrument—you can practice at home, but it really needs an audience.

The gender scene is a love-hate relationship for me. I like going out with good-looking, intelligent people with savvy and style. I don't like being forced against my will into being with a bevy of deadheads. They're just interested in a respectable image, but a woman has the right to be a tramp or a whore. They think that to legitimize transvestism,

Bob, and Bob as Malinda. "The things that make me strongest in my everyday existence as a male are the result of crossdressing."

they all have to emulate the D.A.R.! To me, most TVs are getting into buffoonery. There's no way crossdressing can exist when you take away the sexual element. It would be like a shoe fetishist without high heels. I'm pursuing physical pleasure, experimenting to find my niche.

Before I do my makeup, I shave twice, going with the grain, and I use two new razor blades. I don't shave my body the same way—not that many people see it. When you're sexually turned on, your beard goes bananas, and since dressing is enough to turn most TVs on, the beard usually comes through before the evening is over. After shaving, I give my face a rest and concentrate on my nail polish.

When I start making up I use a cream foundation. It's thicker, more three-dimensional, and it flattens the face. I minimize the jawline, contouring it to give the illusion of being femininely triangular, rather than the masculine square shape. I can't pass as a woman during the day, but sometimes I can at night. I go for glamour, and I use theatrical makeup. I always get a lot of strokes for my makeup. It brings out the artist in me. It causes sadness, too. I'm like Cinderella: I went to the ball, but then I have to wash it off.

For Malinda's breasts, I take a cup and a quarter of birdseed, and put it in a double thickness of pantyhose. Then I tie it off. The package is fairly heavy and somewhat pliable, and I turn the knot toward the front to make the nipple bulge. If I want a size 38-DD, I just add more birdseed. It's an occupational hazard if a flock of birds happens along while you're walking in the park!

It takes me about two hours to complete the process of becoming Malinda. I don't feel like a different person as Bob or Malinda, but I've grown a lot in my male role since coming out as a TV. I've become bolder, more aggressive, more masculine in a way.

I feel as if I've eaten of the tree of knowledge, and others are just wandering out in the garden someplace. I've tasted the poison fruit. People think that by crossdressing I've been able to get some penetrating insights into being a woman. They give me too much credit. The things that I may have learned by going out dressed as a stereotypical female are things that benefited me more as a male. I've learned to master fear, to be self-reliant, to be aggressive and dominant. The things that make me strongest in my everyday existence as a male are the result of crossdressing.

When I'm Malinda, I sometimes think, Well, they might not notice my "Come Fuck Me" heels, but they'll notice my eyes . . . I know how to do eyes. But even with all my skill, sometimes I still see a sadness there. I guess there aren't enough skirts and dresses in the whole world to cover the lonely spot in the center of my heart.

I remember walking down the center of Commercial Street in Provincetown at four A.M., dead drunk, with my heels in one hand, swinging my purse in the other. The officers in the parked car smile and wave as I walk past. I look into the mirror when I get back to the hotel, the tears start. But tomorrow is another day. I am invited to a champagne party at a leather bar for gay men. I remember thinking, Maybe I'll get lucky and meet somebody worthwhile on the dance floor. Maybe I'll get lucky and find some tenderness and romance.

Bob becoming Malinda. "I start with a cream foundation. It's thicker, more three-dimensional, and it flattens the face."

"I get a lot of strokes for my makeup. It brings out the artist in me."

"When I was growing up, often I would stare deeply into the mirror and ask, 'Why?' Thirty years later I look into the mirror and ask the same question."

Rachel and Malinda, backstage at the Fan Fair Follies

"If I want a size 38DD, I just add more birdseed."

Bob, and Bob as Malinda with girlfriend Janet

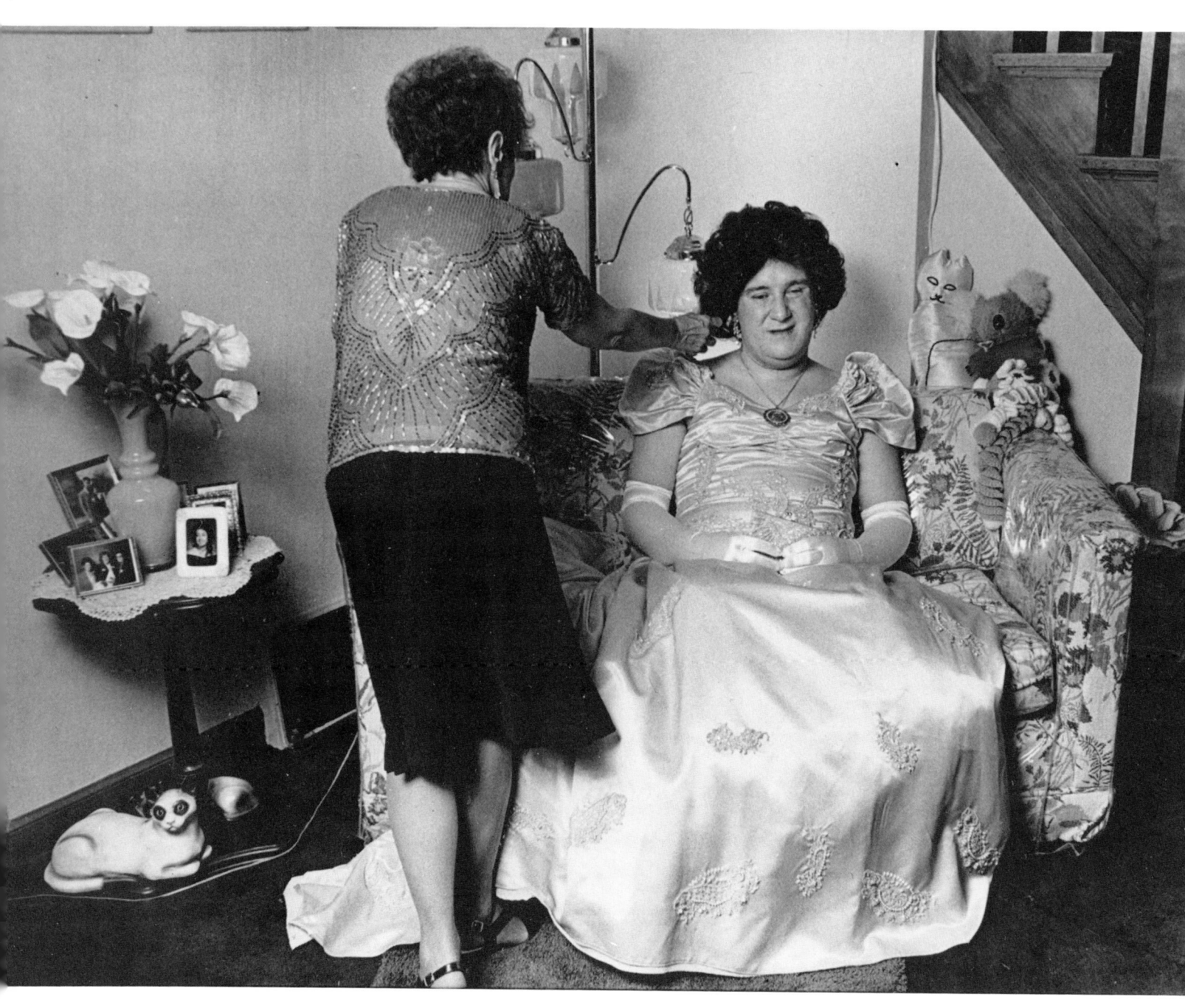

Elizabeth Anne being primped by Mom. "My father thought all boys should be good at is science and math, not gingerbread and frills."

ELIZABETH ANNE

Ever since I was little, I was a creative person, with a talent in art. Born visually impaired, later my hearing was damaged by measles. My father feared injury if I learned to work with tools, so although he was an electrician, he refused to teach me his trade. I started crossdressing when I was eight. My mother knew about it from the beginning and kept it from my father, a macho man, who thought all boys should be good at science and math, not gingerbread and frills. I was afraid of my father, and I had nightmares of him catching me in women's clothes.

I have always liked and appreciated beautiful clothes. I was initially inspired by the old movies our family would watch on television. When I was older, I heard about the work and image of women's clubs: the fancy teas, installations, tours of historic homes. I had an installation gown made resembling one worn by a past president of a garden club. After about five years of struggle, I joined a women's garden club, entered several shows, and won some prizes in flower arranging. I joined three different churches to find one that would allow me to take part in its women's circle.

When I joined Tri-Ess, I was able to dress fully, but the club was far from what I expected, because I believe in acting my full femme-self. The femme role is not talking in a singsong voice, or about makeup. It is a woman's sense of caring; it is higher goals. Our meetings should be run like women's clubs, with uplifting programs on the arts or community service, encouraging the talent of members and even featuring such extras as a fancy refreshment table. Wearing women's clothing is an art form, and my association with women has allowed my creativity to reach its full potential. My crossdressing is a legitimate hobby and a tribute to real women.

KARY

After we each got divorced, Laura and I lived together for two or three years before I told her about my desire to crossdress. She was flabbergasted. I gave her things to read, and she became accepting in the bedroom, but not out of the house. At that time I was satisfied with getting dressed for sexual gratification. We discovered that she gets quite horny when she makes me up.

When I was trying to get Laura to accept my dressing, I got her into a little light domination. She would tie me up and force me to get dressed. Now, if we weren't into crossdressing, we might still be into bondage. She's really gotten into it. One time, she made me put on a bra, garter belt, stockings, an androgynous top, and women's blue jeans, and we went out shopping with the kids. Another time, I came home early from work and she tied me to the bed while she went out to pick the kids up from school. When she came back, we made mad, passionate love. Most of the time we make love—as Bob, or even as Kary—we end up making love the usual way. I'm very happy with my relationship, and I wouldn't want to do anything to change it. If anything ever happened to Laura, I don't think I'd ever find anyone else who could accept me; I might take hormones, but I'd never have a sex change. The image of the she-male intrigues me. It's the best of both worlds. It's another way of expressing Kary. A complete male-female . . . by yourself.

Three years ago, my dad died at the age of fifty-three. I looked at my life and thought I was hiding half of it. I didn't want to live the rest of my life in the closet. If he died at that young an age, when am I going to go? I wanted to take Kary out of the house. This was a very hard time for Laura. Finally, she agreed to go with me to my first Crossroads meeting. We became very active in the club, and I think if I were to die tomorrow, Laura would seek out another crossdresser. She feels we are more sensitive, caring, open-minded, and nonjudgmental.

LAURA (KARY'S MATE)

I had a horrible marriage, then Kary came back into my life, a very caring person. I feel lucky. The disadvantage of being with Kary is that we have to be careful around my ten-year-old son.

Bob/Kary at work

Dana and her father, Kary

I've always been the dominant figure in the relationship, and he would really like me to do it all the time, even at work—call him up and dictate to him. He's a very passive person but also has the capacity to take the man's role. He's dominant every once in a while if he disagrees with me, like the period we were negotiating about his wearing a nightgown to bed. I told him that on the nights I wasn't going to school, he would be Bob and not wear a nightgown. He said, "Sure," but then he acted as if every time he was Bob we'd have sex. I felt guilty about saying no. Now he wears his nightgown every night and I don't say a word about it. Two years ago that really bothered me. Now I'm used to it. I lost that negotiation.

DANA (KARY'S DAUGHTER)

This last summer, I turned fourteen, and decided I wanted to live in Detroit with my dad and Laura and go to Catholic school. Two weeks before Halloween, Dad came into my room. He had a nightgown on. I thought it looked kind of funny and I kind of snickered a little bit, but he's my dad and no matter what he is, I still love him. If he had a sex change, I'd still love him. That's all there is to it.

In my other school, the kids talked about gays and transvestites, so I knew about it. Before I came here, Dad called my mom and told her about his crossdressing. She got off the phone and was in shock, and I asked her what was wrong. She said, "Your dad is a transvestite! What is that?" I explained it to her.

Laura, Kary, and Laura's mother. Kary: "I think if I were to die tomorrow, Laura would seek out another crossdresser. She feels we are more sensitive, caring, open-minded, and nonjudgmental."

MERISSA

I've been dressing all my life, ever since I realized that little girls are treated better than little boys. I became very friendly with my sister's delectable calico dress. I was also big on pillowcases. Nobody could understand why mine always had holes in them: they make very nice little dresses when you're four years old. By the time I was thirteen I was a confirmed crossdresser. I'd gone through the emotional rewards as a little kid; sensually, it just felt good, and then it became a turn-on. When you combine those elements, it gets deeply rooted in the soul. I got caught once by my parents, and was beaten with a rubber hose. I was treated with indifference from childhood on, and learned that the opposite of love isn't hate, it's indifference. It wasn't that they really gave a damn about me; they were concerned about what would happen if the neighbors ever saw me.

My parents were successful in teaching me the fear of social reprisal. The next twenty years of my life were miserable, trying to be what everybody else said I was supposed to be. In high school I held five school records in track and field. I joined Special Forces, got into reconnaissance, was sexually active, all the appropriate images. I went to college as a philosophy major, mostly trying to make sense out of what was going on inside me, and taught skiing for eight years. I found my happiness in the wilderness, where nobody questioned my gender.

When I was thirty-three, my father died and I came out of the hills to take care of the trailer park that he owned—where I grew up. I was out there, without a shirt, all hairy and bearded, when a gal I'd never seen before came up to me and asked if I thought she was attractive. We marched back to her trailer, she took me to her bedroom, and showed me six feet of negligees. I demonstrated an above average interest in her closet, and she picked up on it. She liked men sexually, but she didn't like men. I, too, had no use for men, I didn't even like being one! So we started to put the pieces of our lives together. Up to this point, I had never loved anyone, least of all myself. I gave her a love she would not have received, and she saved my life. Three years later she died of leukemia.

Merissa—Philosopher. "When we're talking about good and evil, right or wrong, masculine and feminine, these are value judgments. They don't exist in nature."

Merissa Sherill Lynn—Founder of the International Foundation for Gender Education

After Sherry died, I was ready to skip the "Me Tarzan, you Jane" nonsense and figure out what I was going to do with my life. I saw my life in terms of a contribution—the best thing I could do would be in the field of gender education. There are not just thousands of people out there, there are millions, and very few people are doing anything for them. So I started working on behalf of the crossdressing and transsexual community out of a sense of duty, and it's that sense of duty that has protected me from burnout.

We started the Tiffany Club in 1977, to support and educate the gender community and serve the northeast region of the United States. By 1981, we started working on *Tapestry,* which is a magazine dedicated to tying together the various gender organizations around the world. Then we formed I.F.G.E., which is the International Foundation for Gender Education, and is intended to be a unifying factor. It sponsors Tapestry Publications, the community's publishing house, and holds annual national conventions that serve all our people.

I've found through working with the crossdressing and transsexual community that there is a great deal of transition. People are in, people are out, and people will use people. I do not believe in "A friend in need is a friend indeed," because everyone is a friend in need. Friendly acquaintances are very easy to come by, but friends are not. I'm loyal and dedicated to my friends, so I have to be very picky in the community as to who becomes my friend. A sense of family is developing within the community, and that's my family now.

Language is a creation itself; it has no existence in nature. So when we're talking about good and evil, right or wrong, masculine and feminine, these are value judgments. They don't exist in nature. What works is love, loving the people whose lives you affect, loving yourself, being in harmony with yourself, not this persona created to satisfy somebody else, but the person that you are. When you enter a rose garden, what is the sensation you have when you touch a rose and feel yourself in that rose? A sense of oneness, harmony with the environment. Now, you take someone inclined as I am to put on a beautiful negligee, something soft and delicate, and you allow yourself to not think but to feel, and you can feel yourself into what you are wearing. You can start crying right on the spot. Crossdressing, when it's used right, becomes a tool for happiness. In crossdressing, if you are aware of the sensations you are experiencing, you can feel yourself walking down the street, you feel your internal poetry, like a dance. This is a religious experience. Something very beautiful, a sensation of life.

Son-in-law Brian, wife Lois, daughter Nancy, and Penny on KP after a church supper

PENNY

I didn't put on a complete outfit until somewhere in my thirties. You can thank *Penthouse* magazine for that. One of their letters to the editor suggested that if you're going to dress, you might as well dress all the way. So I figured, Why not give it a whirl? That brought about a real guilt trip. It was as if I crossed the border of something. I didn't doubt I was a man, but I knew "real" men didn't wear women's clothes. For the next fifteen years I crossdressed very rarely. I buried it. It came up again when my wife and I were not getting along. By then, I knew what transvestism was, but I still didn't know I was one. I started dressing again. I'd come to a resurrection. Lois and I weren't progressing down the primrose path too well, so I dropped the bomb. We talked about it. Some laughs, some cries, and then we hit the pits.

I don't know what's down the road. Our problems are intimacy and community. Lois doesn't want Penny in the bedroom, and I don't know if our community wants Penny anywhere.

When we were first married, Lois had your basic wardrobe: white bra, white pants, white garters. I started buying her colors, some lacy things, pretty underwear, nothing outrageous. At the time I wasn't thinking, I wish I could wear that. Later I did.

Sometimes I have a question as to who's doing the screwing, and I'm picturing myself in the opposite role. In life I'm a doer, I don't like being "done," except under those circumstances.

As Penny, I feel separate from the rest of the world, as if I didn't have a care. I don't have any problems with the masculine role, although sometimes I feel like saying, "Lay off, will you!" Emotionally, I think men would live longer, and women be less threatened during periods of stress, if we didn't have to behave differently. Stress puts women on a guilt trip more than it does men. Men bury stress. That's what I used to do.

LOIS (PENNY'S WIFE)

About fifteen years ago, Bill tried to tell me about the crossdressing, but he didn't know what it was. I was working from three to eleven in the evening and he told me that he'd put on my underclothes then. I immediately went into two weeks of grieving before I finally

came back to my senses. I decided that the poor thing missed me so much, that he needed to put on some of my clothes. I never saw it as anything but a sexual need for me!

He saw to it that I had the most beautiful lingerie. When the catalogs would come, he'd ask me what I liked, and if I was hesitating between two colors, he'd get me both! I remember seeing something on television about transvestites and thinking, How strange! But I never suspected him.

We'd been married for over twenty-five years when Nancy, our youngest, left home in '79. Bill brought home a book, *TV-TS: Mixed Views*. After I'd read it, he said, "That's what I am." I asked him to throw it away. I didn't want to have anything to do with it.

We went to a counselor and I just accepted what the counselor said—that he would be dressing, and it *had* to be OK with me. We decided by the end of the summer that I had it down pat. That January I tried to commit suicide. I ran as far as I could in a snowstorm, hoping the cold would get me. From then until sometime after October was the roughest time in our lives. I couldn't stand to have sex with him. I was really threatened, and never knew if he was seeing himself as a man or a woman. I really didn't want to have sex with a woman.

Bill went to a crossdressing event in Provincetown for the first time that June. When he came back he was wearing a little chain and had a vibrant, bubbling sparkle in him that I hadn't seen in years. I realized that crossdressing did it for him, and I didn't. I thought, It's over with us. I moved into the trailer down the hill, within view of our house. Then my supervisor, who knew the whole story, suggested I go to P-town for Fantasia Fair. I joined the wives' support group, and our stories were so similar, it could have been a broken record. It was after that workshop that Bill and I finally got back together, which is why we wear two wedding rings.

NANCY (PENNY'S DAUGHTER)

Four years ago, when I was twenty, Mum and Dad decided to tell us girls the big secret. We went out to dinner. Mum was nervously fidgeting all over the place, and Dad was grinning from ear to ear. He said, "I'm a crossdresser." I was a little shocked. I still have a hard time understanding it, but for him it's such a special thing.

For a time, I accepted the fact that he dressed and I accepted the fact that I did not want to see him dressed. I mean, he's always been my *daddy*. A daddy is a daddy; he's not a daddy in ladies' clothes. But after hearing about how much fun Fantasia Fair is, I said, "Mum, slip me a couple of Daddy's pictures, and don't tell him." I looked at them and thought, This isn't so bad.

I attended the Fair and could see that my father wasn't the only odd duck in the world. I was so glad I was there for the fashion show. The models needed all the hints you could give them; it was like taking the hand of a little sister.

My dad and I have always been pretty close, and when he first told me that evening with Mum, he said, "I love you, and I'm still just as much a man." That made everything OK with me. They are the parents I would have picked.

Lois and her husband, Penny. Lois: "I joined the wives' support group, and after that Bill and I got back together, which is why we wear two wedding rings."

SHEILA

My mother had a pair of red satin pumps that I adored. I wore them as often as I could. I remember one day she was looking for me, and I was trapped in her closet with those shoes on. I moved to the back of the closet and stood there, way behind her clothes. I felt very close to my mother as I was growing up. She was a very sensual woman, dressed beautifully. She had control over people just by her warmth and her personality. She could walk into a room and capture that room. So when she said to me, "You might make a good physician," I believed it.

My first rotation as an intern was in pediatric services, where I observed a lot of severe illness and death. I was stunned by that. The next service was OB/GYN. That was full of brightness and happiness. The physician is really giving something to his patients. In obstetrics you say, "Here is your son, or here is your daughter." I found that glorious. I would sometimes get choked up with that experience. I think that I can relate very strongly to women.

After my training I got a position in a hospital, and my wife and I moved. She came across some of my things, very nicely wrapped and boxed. She challenged me and asked if I was gay, and was I dating men. We talked about it, but never could work it out very well. I once suggested that I'd like to go as a female to a Halloween party we were invited to. After a lot of urging, she went in a tuxedo, and I wore a gown. My great joy was going into that party with all those good friends and being exhilarated by the surprise and excited comments made by many of the men about how my hair looked and my clothing fit, and where did I get that shoe size? As the evening wore on, people started to get out of their costumes, and my wife suggested I do that, too. I wasn't about to.

Sheila—Obstetrician. "In obstetrics I say, 'Here is your son,
or 'Here is your daughter.' I find that glorious.
I sometimes get choked up with that experience."

Sheila getting dressed to go out

My second marriage was to a young woman who learned about Sheila on another Halloween. I suggested that we each wear a surprise costume and have our own party. I put on a beautiful black gown, took two bottles of champagne, knocked on her door, and said, "Here's the treat, I'm the trick." She roared! She thought it was fantastic! After a while she said, "Anyone who puts on makeup as well as you do has been putting it on for a long time," so I told her all about it. We talked for about a week. She tried so hard to work it out in her mind. Finally she did a tremendous turnabout. She bought lingerie and makeup for Sheila, and took pictures of me. For the next six months, she was so involved with Sheila that I became frightened. I thought it was a little too much, but I bought this house and we got married. After a month, she did a one-hundred-and-eighty-degree turn. Told me my friends were faggots, and I mustn't do this any longer. I learned through mutual friends that she said she was going to change me. That brought out such anger in me that within a couple of months we separated.

I'm in my mid-fifties and soon I will have taken care of my three children and their educational needs. During the last six weeks, after considering my general health, I put myself on hormones. About seven years ago, I had a brief moment of use for three months. I was in an unhappy time of my life, and I wanted to do it, but I knew it wasn't the time. This time I know it is. I think if I have cosmetic or plastic surgery done, I might have breast implants, but I don't think I would ever go beyond that. I'm fascinated by the female breast. My mother had a splendid, very full-breasted figure. My fascination with breasts started there.

I feel that I am maturing and progressing all the time in my feminine role, not just in physical ways, but in terms of feminine considerations. I'm very committed to giving of myself to the community. I like to give seminars, I like to write to other TVs and introduce them to the community. I see the remainder of my life in that manner, being committed to the feminine role and helping others come as far as they want to come. After giving up OB/GYN, I will continue to practice medicine as a consultant to members of my community in the area of gender, advising individuals in the pre-op transsexual aspect of their lives. I will live and practice as Sheila.

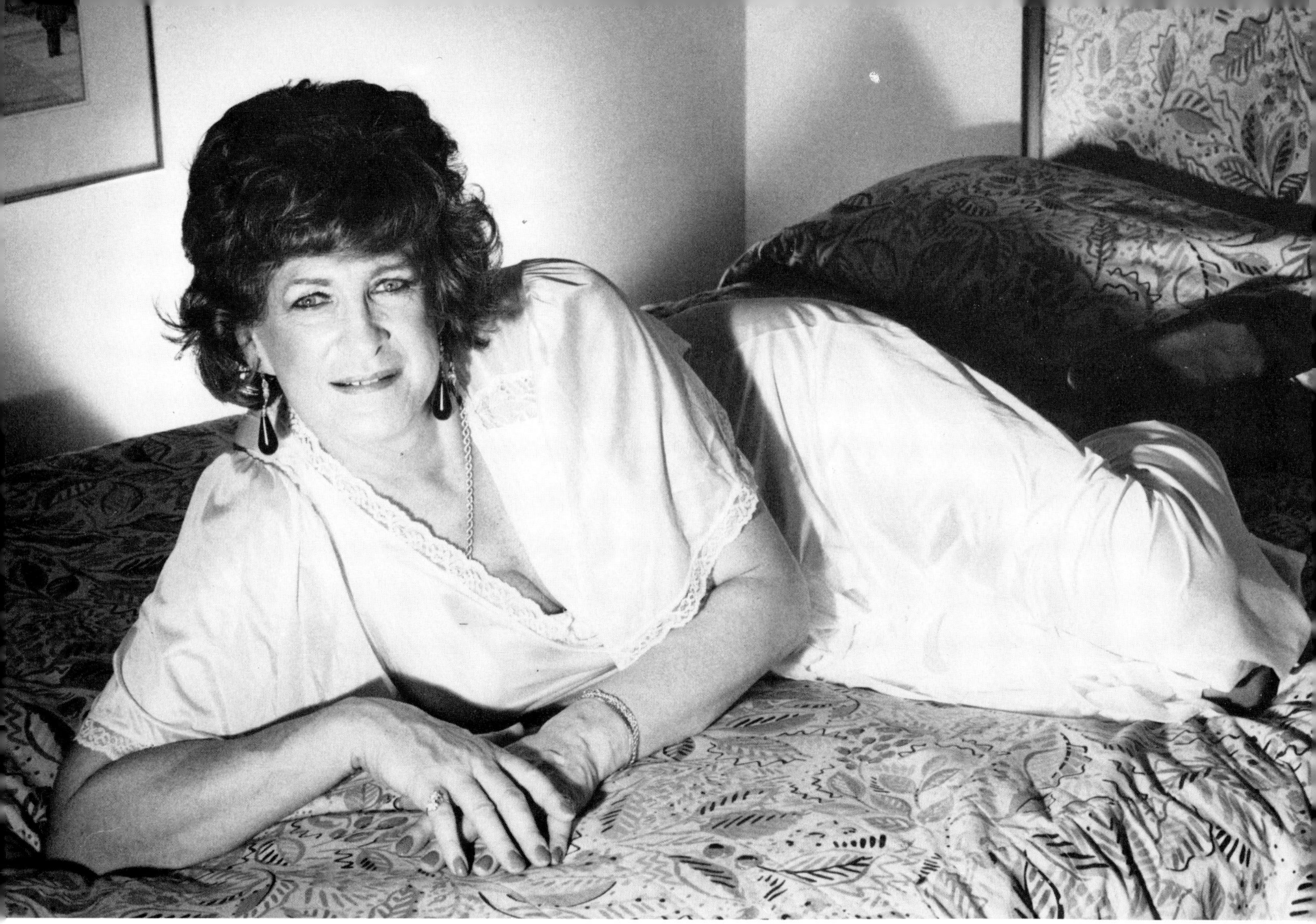

Sheila lounging

Sheila moved by a church service

DAVIDA

What I've always admired about women, they can just break down and cry in front of anybody and it's okay. Men really can't do that without being labeled weak. Women's emotions can flow all the time. When I'm dressed as Davida, or especially when Corinne is dominating me, I can express my emotions freely.

A turning point in my crossdressing came when I met Corinne. I'd been reading about dominant women, and it really excited me, but I couldn't share that with anyone. She said, "You know, I've always wanted a man I could dominate and feel easy around. Instead of having men putting pressure on me, and being in control, I'd like to be in control." That really excited me, so one time, she dressed me up in some of her clothes. That she was doing it to me was the exciting part; it was sending me to outer space. When you've been a powerful man all your life, and you're brought into a position where you're completely hooked, helpless, in clothes that are impractical, that have no function except to entice, that excites me.

I've always had a foot fetish, and high heels to me are like bikinis for the feet. I admire real glamour, like that of Rita Hayworth, Greta Garbo, Marlene Dietrich. They were gorgeous women, they slinked across the screen, sex dripping off them. They were so powerful, everybody just worshiped them. Men were at their feet. Now that's the fantasy of glamour. That's the kind of thing I'd like to be, as much as I could, considering I'm a man.

Davida and mate, Corinne. Davida: "When I'm dressed as Davida, or especially when Corinne is dominating me, I can express my emotions freely."

Davida and Corinne

RHONDA

I believe that if society were more open to men wearing women's clothes, if you could just go out in public and not worry about starting a ruckus, there would be a certain number of us who would not dress to "pass." I'm a blend of male and female—like a culotte. It has legs like pants and the flair of a skirt. If I could wear what I wanted, I would probably wear skirts or culottes with my business suit top, and maybe some heels and jewelry. Wearing women's clothes is escapism, comfort, and tranquillity. If I want to relax, all I have to do is get into "more comfortable" clothing, and all the worries of the world go away.

We had a big old empty attic and there was a trunk of discarded clothing. That was my refuge and my play area and that's where I tried on the stockings. One thing I cannot do without is pantyhose. I wear it virtually twenty hours a day, seven days a week.

In the area in which I grew up, in northern Wisconsin, part of a boy's reaching adulthood consisted of being allowed to handle a gun and go hunting with the men. That happened to me when I was around ten. It was a cold and rainy day, and we were to go bird hunting. My father insisted that I go and dress warmly, but I couldn't find any warm underwear. After a lot of looking around, my mother finally found a pair of my sister's tights. When I objected to wearing them, my father pulled my pants down and spanked me in front of everyone. It was a very painful, traumatic, humiliating experience. Thereafter, I developed a compulsion to wear tights.

Dad has never known how to be affectionate. I can see the sensitivity and the love in him, but as a kid, there were many times I didn't like him.

I was well into dressing before I had sex on my mind. My best friend, who was a couple of years older than me, taught me to masturbate. After that, he wanted to practice having sex with girls, so he fucked me between my legs. This caused me some confusion later on, in junior high.

On the day my wife decided to kick me out, I finally told her about my cross-dressing. We sought counseling for our marital problems, and she took me to a Tri-Ess meeting. I've since shared this with a close male friend and my regional sales manager. I've been happier since I started sharing. Each time I tell another person, I feel like I've gotten rid of a load of pressure. You make your own prison in your mind.

Randy and sister, Claudia

SUE (RHONDA'S WIFE)

When I first heard about Rhonda I was numb. That was due to lack of knowledge, and Randy had little knowledge to offer me. Emotionally, it took two years to get to the point of neutrality about it. I do not find Rhonda sexually exciting. I do not find Rhonda a turn-off. Rhonda just exists. Intellectually, I don't find Rhonda particularly delightful, but I don't find her unacceptable either. Rhonda is an extension of Randy and most of the time it doesn't matter to me which one it is except, of course, sexually. Then it's just Randy. I sleep with Rhonda—I do not make love to Rhonda. When Randy wants to make love, he comes to bed in male clothes. There are nights when I'm glad to see a nightgown, 'cause there's just no way I'm in the mood! It's not all bad.

I guess acceptance has to be based on two things—one is the type of person Rhonda is. Granted, there are times I wish Rhonda would go away . . . there are times I wish Randy would go away! For the most part, I don't feel put upon by Rhonda. She gets a lot of money spent on her, but that isn't a financial drain.

Shopping for women's clothes for him and for me are two very different things. Our tastes, our sizes, and our palettes are different. I don't share his clothes, although I'm constantly borrowing his black slip because I don't have one, but I can't wear his black bra because it's padded. This is one level of acceptance.

The second part of acceptance has to do with me and who I am. I do not focus my world around anyone else. I share my world with those I love, but I am the center of my world. What if he had told me about his crossdressing before we were married? I didn't have ten years, two kids, a house in the suburbs, a station wagon, and a garage. I mean all that sounds crass, but that's a fact. Would I opt to take on this situation, all else being equal? Hell no! Why add one more aggravation to the pile? But if you say to me, "Would you trade a loving, sensitive, conscientious TV for Joe Macho?" Hell no, either! That's not the kind of man that appeals to me. I came to the realization long ago that if we ever split up, it won't have anything to do with his being a TV.

Randy as Rhonda, with Claudia. Rhonda: "I'm a blend of male and female, like a culotte."

ROBIN

I've been crossdressing as far back as I can remember. Ma was the worst dresser in the world. I didn't even like her clothes. I started working when I was fifteen. I'd call and order things from Ward's catalog, and they'd think I was picking them up for Ma. She'd find the suitcase I used for collecting things and she'd dump the clothes, but she never said a word to me. I wish she would have said something.

I would have loved to get a doll when I was a kid. They were shoving fishing, sports at me. I got pushed to play basketball. I did not enjoy sports. I would have loved to learn to sew, to learn to cook. I got into a lot of fighting, and was the little terror of the block. My brother was twice my size, but he wouldn't get into a quarter of the fights I got into.

After I graduated from high school, I went to trade school and became a skilled journeyman. I got married at nineteen. I thought that was going to cure the problem. It didn't, and I started drinking as an escape. I'd fall over drunk in the parking lot. I thought of doing myself in a couple of times. I could never talk to my wife. I thought I was the only one in the world who crossdressed, and that there was something drastically wrong with me. I'd go fishing, to try and get my mind off it. I had a horrendous temper. If anybody said anything bad to me, they'd be lying on the floor. I tried to get rid of these feelings, but they would always come back. I had a few feminine things; my wife would find them and throw them away. I'd fish them out of the garbage, and throw them in the company truck. When I was out of town I would wear them. These feelings run deep. I think you're born with them.

I knew Cecile before we each divorced. Her husband and I had been friends through the CB radio, and she and I spoke frequently. We'd talk to each other about our problems, although I never brought up the crossdressing on the radio. Cecile and I got married, were happy together, but I felt I had to talk to another crossdresser. The first time I ever saw another one was on "Phil Donahue." Then I saw someone on "Twin Cities Live" and we arranged to meet. The next night, she took us to a female impersonator show, and the crossdresser club party the night after that. Three nights of openness. I felt great. I was flying the whole week, and it was after that I decided to tell the kids. I just felt I wasn't going to hide it from them anymore. We asked them if they wanted to see the bedroom and Robin's clothes, and then we hugged. I had never really hugged them all those years. Not what I call a sincere hug.

Robin's personality goes right with Ralph's now. All the guys at work have seen the difference. I used to go in grouchy. Since I told the girls, I go in with a smile ninety-nine percent of the time. Even if it's six-thirty in the morning. It's hard to get me angry. Someone at the club put me in touch with a makeup company, and now both Cecile and I do makeup classes and sell their products. Women love to get made up by me. I work as Walter. Now I have two jobs: makeup and construction. I also make breast forms and design jewelry. I'd like to design for crossdressers—large bangle bracelets are hard to find! I wish society would accept us. I'd just like to blend in.

Robin with daughters and second wife, Cecile. Robin: "I'd call and order things from Ward's catalog, and they'd think I was picking them up for Ma."

Vicky doing the can-can with the author's children, Cori and Julia

VICKY

When I was four or five, I loved to play with a pink slip. I don't know what possessed me. It was hanging on a line and it was gorgeous! I saw a full-page illustration in *Life* magazine of Rita Hayworth kneeling in bed, wearing a pink negligee with a bodice of black lace, and I made a drawing of it. Even though I was so young, I was turned on—I wanted to be her. One time I played with a boy who tried to have sex with me in a peanut patch. I was the girl. It was scary and exciting. When I was thirteen or fourteen, I accumulated a cache of clothing, a nightgown here, a bra there. My mother discovered the cache and thought the clothes were souvenirs from sexual exploits, but all during puberty, when I went to bed at night, I'd pray that I would wake up and be a girl, even for a day.

I had just finished the Army when I discovered an ad for Virginia Prince's organization for TVs. They had a social once a month where you could not come dressed, but you could bring a pair of heels and hose in a bag. The first time I dressed fully was when I met some of the people from this group. Shortly after that, I stopped working as an engineer and went to art school. I came across *Drag* magazine, and I started doing the covers and illustrated stories. I was hoping for another *Vogue*—images of transvestites enjoying themselves, trying on clothes. All the expression was positive.

Since sex has been taken out of the equation due to the AIDS epidemic, much of the enjoyment of impersonating a woman has become kind of academic. I'm not a queen, but I hate the words "transvestite" or "crossdresser"; they're too clinical. People probably think of me as a snob, but I like being a whore, too, being very sexy, running around in a transparent blouse. I've been to some clubs where I have ended up on stage doing a slow striptease. I am quite pleased to be exhibitionistic in a transparent petticoat, but if I'm walking down Fifth Avenue, I do it in high style, as I did recently at the Copacabana in an evening gown. I'm always trying to get a reaction. My desire is to be an exceptional, ebullient, well-liked, and, if possible, pretty woman.

I had a ten-year relationship with a woman. The dressing was nice, as far as she was concerned, as long as it was just play. I'd go take the garbage out in my nightgown and try to make it to the incinerator and back; there was adventure and she was part of it. But when I started going to balls and to Mardi Gras, she sat home envisioning all sorts of sex. And when I'd come home and want to be Vicky, she felt I was more glamorous than she was. She wondered if she was lesbian. It got to be stressful for her and we broke up. I don't blame her.

The men I've lived with were gay lovers. Gay men, almost routinely, don't wish to think about drag, except recently, with the AIDS epidemic, guys are doing drag as something else to do, another avenue of expression. Because of the epidemic, there's a dearth of sexy socializing, and drag has filled in more and more. The Halloween parade is bigger. Gays are wearing drag on Fire Island. Before, they looked down on it. Just as my girlfriend was, gays are put off by femininity, by the lack of the macho image. It's not exclusively an aversion to heterosexuals, it's an aversion to homosexuals, too, but now since they're not having sex, it's not as upsetting. Lingerie becomes a play item.

What kills me is that gay people have forgotten the accomplishments of the Stonewall riot, a turning point in gay history. Coming out, year after year, unaware that transvestites were the ones that started the riot. I'm not political, but I very much admire those who are, and I believe that transvestites should be proud and should be honored for what they've accomplished. Because when you do drag, when you dress to express yourself as a woman, you're totally without façade. You're utterly vulnerable, you're not protecting yourself. You're carrying your feelings not only on your sleeve, but all over you.

Vicky applying her nails in Provincetown *Out of one world, and into another*

Vicky in vinyl heaven

RENÉE

When I was seven or eight, I got into a bag of my cousin's clothes. I climbed up to look in the mirror and thought I looked pretty sitting on the dresser in the red and white dress. I was comfortable, and felt warm and good.

When I was young, I was trying to be perfect, trying to be the kid my parents wanted. My father was absent most of the time. He was a barge captain, and after work he'd get drunk and stay out with the boys. My mother would welcome him home with open arms, screams, and shouts. As I got older, I tried on my cousin's and my mother's clothes once in a while, and it became very sexually gratifying. In eighth grade I switched from Catholic to public school, and it put me into the male world of having to make my place, and I learned to fight. I didn't have any sexual relations until I was in the service.

I found a magazine that had an article on Christine Jorgensen. That interested me because I felt trapped in the wrong body. At that time, I would have jumped at the chance to have sex reassignment. I would put on lipstick and a babushka and my mother's clothes and squeeze into her shoes, and walk around the house for ten or twenty minutes. Before dressing I was excited, and I would hold on to myself so nothing was let loose. Afterward, I felt bad and very guilty.

I was drafted, and wound up in Vietnam. I was there for nine months, so stoned that I could hardly see. When I got home, all I wanted was to forget about it, so I took a menial job and tried to crossdress as much as possible. It was the sixties, miniskirts were the rage, and I just wanted to blend in, but I looked like a buffoon. We've had our battles, the mirror and I.

Renée and Kevin taking their vows

Renée and Kevin with members of the wedding party and the minister

The reception

Renée and Kevin. Renée: "We were in love with each other, and it didn't matter what clothes I wore."

"All through the years we're raised to end up either men or women, to be separate. It's an artificial thing that someone else created, and I can't live there."

Finally I met a girl, loved everything about her, and we were married eight months later. After four years, I told her about my crossdressing and she saw me dressed. I was running around thinking I was a transsexual and that I had to do something about it. I started on hormone therapy, taking as much as I could get, and began formulating what kind of woman I would be. I went to TVIC [Transvestite International Club] meetings and spent time talking to transsexuals, but found I really didn't fit in with them at all. By this time, my wife was on the verge of moving out. I was depressed about everything, and the hormones weren't helping. I had a final confrontation with my wife, and then tried to drown myself in the icy Hudson River. I ended up swimming to shore. I took the clothes I had in the car, and forty dollars, and hopped a bus to New York.

I got a room in Hell's Kitchen and a job as a waitress in a greasy spoon near Times Square. I was doing pretty well living as a woman, but miserably as far as life went. One day I was at work and some guy gave me a hard time, so I turned around and punched him! I realized then that there was still a lot of Rich around. I quit my job, moved out of the hotel, and called my ex-wife, who thought I was *dead*—I had left the car parked by the water!

I moved back, returned to my old job, and my wife and I split up for good. The hormones had taken away my sexual drive, but the desire to crossdress was still there. I went off the hormones and had several relationships until I met Sharon and her kids. I hid the crossdressing from her for four years, again thinking I could conquer it. I felt guilty for hiding my desires from her, and the guilt led to violent temper tantrums. I moved to a motel down the road. I wanted to be free to dress again. After a few days there, I called her and told her about me, and what she might expect in the future. At the end of the week, I called again and she said, "Come on home. We'll work something out." We started going out together as Renée and Sharon on a regular basis, and when I started a new club [Transgenderists International Club], she became active in it, too.

About two years ago, I talked to Sharon about taking hormones again. I said I wanted my femme image enhanced. Sharon agreed to it once she understood that it wouldn't interfere with her sexual pleasure. I can maintain an erection, and she can still have sex whenever she wants. I can sense when she wants it, and I get pleasure out of being very close to her, but I'm not led around by the fact that I have to have sex.

When I was young, I ran around being led by my dick. As I got older, I realized there was more to life than *that*. It was time to figure out whether life was between my legs or between my ears. I found I could combine both of my personas in one being.

Last June, after living together for over eight years, Rich and Sharon got married. And in November, we married again, this time as Renée and Kevin. We were in love with each other, and it didn't matter what clothes I wore. Now Renée, the person I had known always existed, could be real. Here I was, a bride, in a dream that was unfolding. The dream that I'd had many times before. I felt numb from head to toe, but more alive than ever before.

EPILOGUE

In 1970, after living as a man for fifty-five years and being divorced a second time, I sold my business and decided that I knew all I needed to know about being a man and that I'd spend the rest of my life as a woman in order to complete the wholeness of my perception of human life.

It is time for us to think in terms of *men's* liberation, so we're no longer bound by the centuries-old set of behaviors, expectations, requirements, and lifestyles that prevent men from ever realizing our potential. Women have needed liberation *to,* that is, the freedom to do the kind of work that interests them, to learn to stand on their own feet as independent persons, not appendages to some male. Men need liberation *from.* We need to escape from the conceptions of manliness that expect us to always be strong, capable of handling whatever may arise, to be a leader.

Crossdressers of whatever persuasion, straight or gay, transvestites, transgenderists, or transsexuals, are in the vanguard of men's liberation because we have faced that which frightens so many men: our inner femininity. We've met this erstwhile enemy and have made a degree of peace with her. We have given her real time existence and three-dimensional reality, and we enjoy her when she is present. I say, "I have met the enemy and SHE is ME!"

Clothing is an admission ticket to a certain way of life. Women's clothing is a means to an end, not an end in itself. For most crossdressers, the feminine clothing simply gets them out of jail, so they can, for a limited time, be the kind of person they cannot be for the rest of the time. Ideal liberation, for all people, is not to *become* women and men respectively, but to achieve the right to express and enjoy the variety of ways people can approach life without having to deal with the label of "masculine" or "feminine." Gender is an anachronism.

VIRGINIA PRINCE
Publisher of the first magazine for crossdressers
Founder of the first social group for crossdressers